Killing Time

Longarm dropped to the floor and rolled as a lance of flame licked across the room searching for flesh. Searching with the bullet that was its spearhead.

He spun off to the side and came up again with the Thunderer in his hand and spitting fire and smoke right back.

The woman with the carbine—French Annie—took his slug full in the chest and fell backward onto the bed she'd just vacated.

A small red dot between her breasts began to leak blood.

He didn't have time at the moment to worry about the fact that he'd just killed a woman.

Longarm scrambled to his feet and began legging it in pursuit of the man who was behind all this . . .

TABOR EVANS

LONGARM

AND THE MONTANA MASSACRE

J

JOVE BOOKS, NEW YORK

LONGARM AND THE MONTANA MASSACRE

A Jove Book / published by arrangement with
the author

PRINTING HISTORY
Jove edition / February 1991

ISBN: 0-515-10512-0

Jove Books are published by The Berkley Publishing Group,
200 Madison Avenue, New York, New York 10016.
The name "JOVE" and the "J" logo are trademarks belonging to
Jove Publications, Inc.

PRINTED IN THE UNITED STATES OF AMERICA

10 9 8 7 6 5 4 3 2 1

LONGARM

AND THE
MONTANA MASSACRE

Chapter 1

Longarm kicked back from the table with his legs extended and his boots crossed at the ankles. He felt good. His belly was full and his spirits high. Lunch at the cafe a few blocks away from the Federal Building had been satisfying if not particularly exciting. And tonight promised to be plenty exciting.

He tugged the old Ingersoll out of his vest pocket and checked the time. Time enough and more than enough, he decided. He reached for a cheroot, nipped the twist off the end of it, and struck a match alight. He could enjoy this smoke and amble back to the office, pick up those warrants Henry wanted him to serve this afternoon, and get those out of the way in plenty of time to go back to his room, bathe, and change for the evening and pick the lady up. The thing she wanted to hear with that string quartet wasn't supposed to start until eight. And then afterward . . .

Longarm smiled to himself and drew smoke into his lungs. The performances afterward would be the ones of

1

real interest. He could put up with listening to some fiddlers until then. It seemed a fair enough exchange.

A boy came into the cafe, ignored the vacant chairs that were available, and went straight to the man standing behind the counter. He asked something of Harve, and the proprietor turned and pointed toward Longarm. The boy thanked him and hurried across the small room.

"Something I can do for you, son?"

"If you're Marshal Long, there is."

"I'm Deputy Long if that's close enough. The marshal for this here district is William Vail, son, not me." Longarm grinned at him. "But I do thank you for trying to give me the promotion."

"Yes, sir, sorry, sir."

"No harm done. Now what is it I can do for you, son?"

"I have a message, Marshal. Deputy, I mean. For you."

"Mmm?"

"You're to get back to your office right away, sir."

Longarm shrugged and got to his feet. That dang Henry was getting bossy again. Although there for sure wasn't any big rush about those warrants. It was just routine paperwork, after all.

He handed the boy a nickel and thanked him, and reached for his brown Stetson before he dropped a coin onto the table to pay for his dinner.

Longarm waved a friendly good-bye to Harve behind the counter and wandered out onto the sidewalk in no great hurry despite the message.

A lady's shy smile, briefly seen from behind the window of a passing carriage, brought a smile from Longarm in return.

Not that he was particularly vain. Far from it, in fact. He never had understood what the ladies saw in his dark and craggy features that seemed to please them. But he wasn't about to start complaining that it was so.

Deputy United States Marshal Custis Long was tall, with broad shoulders and lean hips. He carried himself with an easy, unaffected grace that seemed to match his looks.

His hair was brown, as was his sweeping mustache, and

2

his face was tanned and weather-worn. He wore a brown tweed coat, brown corduroy trousers, and black stovepipe boots with a military heel. A black gunbelt was visible under the coat, and the butt of a double-action Colt Thunderer was canted at an angle just to the left of his belt buckle, rigged for a cross-draw. The watch chain slung across the front of his vest held the expected pocket watch at one end, but at the other there was no fob. Instead he carried a .41-caliber brass hideout derringer there. Just in case.

The deputy they called Longarm had never thought of himself as being anything or anyone out of the ordinary. Just a man doing a job that he was good at.

And if that job involved rambling around Denver serving warrants for petty infractions of obscure laws, well, that was what he would have to do today. Tomorrow things might get interesting again.

He touched the brim of the flat-crowned Stetson toward the lady whose coach was rumbling down the street and smiled again.

He walked down to the corner and turned onto Colfax, past the Mint with its blue-uniformed, shotgun-bearing guards, and on toward the granite steps leading into the Federal Building, where the United States marshal's offices were.

A corridor led him to the outer office where Marshal Billy Vail's clerk sat hunched over his desk with stacks of warrants and newly arrived wanted posters and who knows what else in front of him. Henry was a bear for hard work, yet the bookish, bespectacled clerk never seemed to get ahead of all he had to do. It was no wonder Henry was so thin; he never seemed to take time away from his desk so he could go grab a bite to eat.

Longarm dropped his hat onto a chair seat instead of crossing the room to the coatrack, and shook his head. "You're getting awful impatient these days, ain't you, Henry? I told you I'd get those papers served for you this afternoon. You didn't have to send for me special."

Henry looked up and blinked, light reflecting off the glass in his spectacles and givin him a blank, eyeless look for just a moment there. "Send for you, Longarm? I didn't send for you."

"You didn't? But—"

"Long! Is that you, Long?" The voice boomed out of Billy Vail's private office.

"Right here."

"It's about time you showed up. Get in here."

Henry shrugged and stood, trailing behind Longarm and entering Vail's office without invitation. Henry always took it as a personal affront should anything happen around there without his knowledge.

"What's up, Boss?" Longarm helped himself to a chair in front of Billy's desk, and Henry joined him.

The U.S. marshal for the Denver District was pink-cheeked and balding. He didn't look at all a man of action. Which was the sort of appearance that could be almighty useful since it was so completely deceptive. And so completely untrue. In his day Billy Vail had been one hell of a field man, and he could still more than hold his own. Nowadays, of course, he was mostly confined to a desk while his deputies went out with guns and guts and handcuffs to get that part of the work done.

"You were saying, Boss?" Longarm eyed the growing length of ash on the front of his cheroot. The cuspidor and ashtrays that were usually available seemed to be missing, probably had been carried off to be cleaned, and he didn't want to peeve the marshal by dropping cigar ash on the rug. Longarm leaned forward and tapped them into a coffee cup that had been left on Billy's desk.

"Comfortable now, Long? Is there anything else you need before we get down to business?" Vail glanced at Henry, but did not otherwise acknowledge his clerk's presence. Longarm was beginning to get the impression that something had happened since this morning to put the boss into a testy humor.

"No, sir. Sorry," Longarm said crisply. There were times when it was all right to joke with Billy Vail. This didn't seem to be one of them.

"Good." Billy shot his jaw and scowled. He swiveled

4

his chair around and stared toward the wall while he spoke. "Are you familiar with Marshal Delbert Hall, Long?"

"No, sir."

Billy grunted. Longarm wished he would turn back so Longarm could get a better look at his expressions. "Hall is U.S. marshal in Montana Territory. A fairly recent appointment there. He works out of Helena."

Until recently, Longarm knew, there hadn't been enough people in the northern territory to justify bothering with Justice Department offices there. Federal appointments in that area had tended to be political and for the most part cosmetic. Some years no one bothered to make appointments at all. Longarm hadn't heard anything about this Marshal Delbert Hall to know if he was another political hack or if his job was supposed to be for real.

Billy Vail grunted again but didn't choose to elaborate on that point. "I know you remember a gentleman named Ambrose Warren," he said.

"That I do," Longarm agreed.

Ambrose Warren, called Brose to his face, and frequently Rabbit behind his back because of his protruding front teeth, long ago had been part of Custis Long's education as a young, wet-behind-the-ears new deputy.

The man was, or at least then had been, a robber of stagecoaches and railroad mail cars. He'd bossed a gang of happy-go-lucky murderers who laughed and joked with their victims and playacted at being latter-day Robin Hoods. But who were quick to shoot an innocent victim down in cold blood if they were crossed to the slightest extent.

One of the oddest things about Brose Warren's gang was that there had been two female train robbers who worked with him. Neither of the bloodthirsty girls had ever been caught.

Rabbit Warren had been, though. Longarm still felt like blushing every time he thought about Warren's capture.

The collar had been made by a very young and still-inexperienced Deputy Custis Long. Longarm—he hadn't even earned his nickname at that point—had caught up with Warren in a Cheyenne whorehouse, more by good fortune than good detection, and had gotten the drop on the robber.

Warren had been easygoing and pleasant about the whole thing. He smiled and gave himself up without a fuss, and congratulated Deputy Long on the capture. He held his wrists out to Long so the handcuffs could be applied without resistance.

It was all so easy that Long should have smelled a rat. But he didn't.

Deputy Long holstered his Colt and pulled out his cuffs . . . and found himself looking into the muzzle of a derringer that had appeared in Warren's hand as if by magic. In this case the magic had consisted of a spring-load device strapped to Warren's right forearm.

Warren wasn't teasing about it either. He popped the little gun into his hand and yanked the trigger. There'd been no hesitation whatsoever. And he'd been smiling still when he did it. It was only a misfire that kept Custis Long from taking a slug in the belly that night.

Did Longarm remember Rabbit Warren? Somewhat.

Had he learned from that experience? Damn right.

"Your friend Warren served his time and was released from prison three months ago, turned loose free and clear with ten dollars to put into the pockets of a brand-new suit of clothes. Now he seems to be back in business," Billy Vail said. "And Marshal Hall up in Helena doesn't seem to much give a shit that he is."

Longarm's eyes narrowed. "Tell me more 'bout this, Billy," he said softly.

Chapter 2

While Custis Long had been having his pleasant, solitary lunch and thinking about delights yet to come, Billy Vail had been having a more disturbing experience dining with the United States attorney for the District.

The Attorney General back in Washington never bothered with getting into the details of each and every little crime that took place in the various states and territories. But he did tend to get excited when his own officers acted deaf, dumb, and blind. And of late he had been receiving complaints from citizens in Montana Territory.

"The thing is," Billy said now, turning to face Longarm and Henry again and giving each of them a level gaze, "and if either one of you repeats a word of this I'll have your asses, the Justice Department is concerned. This is an election year, after all, and we could get caught in the middle of it if one party wants to point fingers at the other about this.

"There is a virtual crime wave under way in the Judith

7

Basin, and Marshal Hall doesn't seem to be doing much about it."

Henry examined his fingernails closely. Longarm opened his mouth to ask a question, but Billy cut him short. "We don't know," Billy said, "if Marshal Hall has been compromised in some way or if he's lazy or even just plain stupid. We simply don't know. The Attorney General *wants* to know. *Before* it becomes a political issue. After all, the man is an appointee of the current Administration. They can't duck responsibility for him. But they, um, quite frankly don't want to alienate him and his, um, Eastern friends and supporters either. Not unless they have to. I'm, uh, sure you know what I mean."

Longarm scowled. If there was anything he hated, dammit, it was a case where politics came into the picture. Billy Vail ran an office that didn't give a shit about political influence. And Longarm liked it that way.

Ambrose Warren on the other hand . . . Billy was getting to that, though.

"I am assuming that our old friend Warren is behind the robberies in the Judith Basin," Billy said, "because the methods are familiar right down to the presence of two females in the robbery gang. Not that anyone has seen Warren's face. The robbers are always masked and wearing dusters over their clothing. But they have conducted a series of robberies in the Basin, knocking over stagecoaches, committing murder there, and robbing at least one bank."

"Do we have jurisdiction?" Longarm asked.

Billy nodded. "No question that there is federal jurisdiction. The stagecoach robberies have included mail pouches."

"Excuse me for interrupting," Henry said, "but that doesn't give *this* office jurisdiction. If the robberies were all committed in Montana Territory . . . "

Vail held a hand up to cut him off. "I know, Henry. The U.S attorney and I talked about that. He's already had his law clerk go back through the files on Warren. There is a case still open on the books, a mail robbery

8

a dozen years ago outside Leadville, that was inside our jurisdiction. We're fairly sure Warren participated in that one but we never had the proof on it, and there were plenty of crimes we could prove against him when Longarm brought him in that time. The file on that one was set aside but never officially closed, and Warren wasn't prosecuted for the Leadville incident. It's reaching, of course, but the U.S. attorney will support us in any jurisdictional, mmm, disputes. If it comes to that."

Henry nodded, satisfied.

"So you want me to go up to the Judith and nose around for Ambrose Warren *and* see if there's anything the Administration ought to know about their fair-haired boy in Helena. Is that about it, Billy?" Longarm asked.

"That, uh, is about it."

"But I do have jurisdiction, so I can use my badge up there if I need to."

"If you need to. I, uh, would prefer that you not flash it about too openly, though."

"You want me t' sniff the wind but not let Marshal Hall know that that's what I'm doing," Longarm said. The shape of it was coming a little clearer now.

Billy nodded.

"He won't be able to use the normal expense vouchers," Henry reminded them. "That would be a dead giveaway."

"I already talked to the U.S. attorney about that," Billy admitted. "The Justice Department will authorize a cash draw against expenses. Out of their budget, in fact. A letter of credit will be prepared this afternoon. The bank that was robbed there is a branch bank, not a locally owned one. Affiliated with The Stockmen's and Commercial Bank of Chicago. The chairman of the board of the Stockmen's and Commercial is, uh, close to the Administration. The U.S. attorney assures me that Longarm can draw against a letter of credit there without it arousing comment in the wrong places."

"Meaning in Helena," Longarm said.

"Exactly."

"You know I don't like this kinda shit, Billy."

9

"I don't either, Longarm, but look at it this way. It gives you another crack at Ambrose Warren."

"There is that, isn't there."

"As for Marshal Hall, just don't go up there with any preconceptions. Keep your mind and your eyes open and let things fall as they will. Any political repercussions needn't be your worry."

"I'll do what I can," Longarm promised.

"That's all I ask."

Something else occurred to Longarm, and he asked, "The mail pouches that were stolen in this string of robberies, Billy. They wouldn't have had anything t' do with bank business, would they? Connected with this Chicago bank that we can count on as being friendly?"

Vail smiled for the first time. "There is always the question of whose ox has been gored, isn't there? As for your question, yes, it is the bank that has suffered. Several cash transfer shipments have been taken. I have a file here with the complaints that have been received in Washington. That will give you the details. All of them that are available, anyway."

Longarm grunted and accepted the folder that Billy pushed across the desk toward him. "It'll take me a while to get up there, y'know. There ain't no easy way to go about it unless somebody's been building railroads lately without me knowing about it."

"It's the long way around," Henry offered, "but the quickest route would be by rail east to the Missouri, then a river steamer north. You can go by water up the Missouri to Fort Benton and then travel south overland to the Basin or take a Yellowstone steamer and ride north, whichever way has the more convenient boat schedule. I recommend the Missouri River route because that way you can borrow a horse free of charge from the garrison at Fort Benton."

Sometimes Longarm thought Henry was a walking, talking encyclopedia. But a useful one. "Better avoid the army post," Longarm said. "If I'm supposed to pass myself off as a disinterested party I'd best not show up riding a horse with a U.S. brand on its shoulder. Come to think of it,

10

maybe I'd best borrow me a stock saddle too and stay off the McClellan this trip. Folks tend to look at a fella odd if he rides a military-style ballbuster when he doesn't have to. Maybe I'll call myself a stockman looking for northern graze. I can stop over to the Diamond K spread this afternoon and see does somebody have a spare saddle I can use."

"Handle it however you like and take whatever time you need," Billy said. "But not too much time. The party conventions won't be for a few months yet, but the battle lines are already being drawn in Washington. I'd rather we had this cleared up and ourselves shut of it before they get serious about the politicking."

Longarm stood, taking the file folder with him. "I'd best get busy," he said. "There's a lot to be done before I can leave." Including, he realized unhappily, having to send a note breaking his date for this evening.

"And no time to waste," the marshal added.

Henry stayed behind to talk to Billy about something, and Longarm went out into the larger office to begin studying what little was known about the situation in the Judith Basin.

Chapter 3

Longarm felt mildly uneasy if not exactly uncomfortable. It wasn't like anything was wrong. It was simply that things were . . . different. He found it hard to believe that he had become so dependent on habit. But the evidence was certainly right there, shouting at him from his own reactions to so simple a thing as changing a few articles of clothing.

At the Diamond K the boys had been pleased—so much so that it made him wonder what they weren't telling him— about fitting him out as a cowman in search of new grazing land. They had quickly found an old stock saddle to loan him. Then, getting into a damn near festive spirit about it, they'd just as quickly taken the beat-up old thing away and raided an equipment shed for a much better replacement. The saddle Longarm was carrying now instead of his old and long-accustomed McClellan was a handsomely tooled, custom-made rimfire rig from a saddler in Pueblo. The seat was big enough to lie down in, and a test ride proved the outfit as comfortable as most rocking chairs. Somewhat heavier too.

They'd also scouted out a matching bridle and breast collar and a fancy saddle pad instead of the normal woolen blanket. Longarm felt like he was on his way to a parade when he sat in the rig they'd assembled.

The boys hadn't been satisfied, though, once they'd loaned Longarm the equipment he came for. They'd insisted that if he was going to pass himself off as a cowman, there were inconsistencies in his outfit that had to be dealt with, and they'd pitched in with glee to correct those faults.

First his boots had had to go. A military heel and round toe just weren't in the cards, they'd declared. Not for a prosperous Colorado cowman. So now Longarm was walking around teetering on high, curved heels so that he felt like he was on stilts. The toes of the borrowed boots were obviously designed for killing roaches in tight corners, and the stitching on the uppers was fancier and more colorful than your average whorehouse wallpaper.

Once the boots were exchanged, the boys had declared that no cowman worth his salt would ever dangle a pair of plain and utilitarian army spurs on the hind end of such artwork. So they'd scrounged a set of silver-mounted spurs with Mexican rowels with bell-shaped silver jinglers attached.

By then Longarm had been feeling like a freak in a sideshow. He'd chimed when he walked and felt conspicuous as hell. He had flatly refused to trade in his brown Stetson for the cream-colored ten-gallon job they'd tried to foist off on him. The son of a buck would have made him eight foot tall, minimum, when combined with his own natural height and the unnatural lift already given by the dogger boot heels.

The Diamond K crew had settled for loaning him—practically by force—a chased silver band for the old Stetson.

By then Longarm was already convinced he knew what a circus clown felt like when he walked the streets.

Now, walking the streets in Omaha while he waited for the flat-bottomed river steamer *Joshua C.* to load, it occurred to him that he never had been told just exactly

13

whose stuff this was that he was sporting courtesy of those friendly cowhands.

He was commencing to get the idea that maybe he had become an unwilling participant in a joke that was being pulled on someone else back there at the Diamond K.

Like maybe he'd walked off with somebody's Saturday night best and with neither him nor the real donor the wiser about it.

That would be all right, he supposed, unless he upped and lost some of this expensive shit. He wondered just how loud the Justice Department would squawk about an expense item, say, for the replacement of a hundred-dollar pair of boots. Something like that could cause commotion all the way to Washington.

Too late to be worrying about that now, though. He was a long day's train ride from Denver at this point, and already had his ticket bought for a riverboat jaunt up the Missouri to Fort Benton.

He checked the Ingersoll for the time. Not that he had to be in any particular hurry. Passengers could board the *Joshua C.* anytime after five o'clock and sleep aboard. The sidewheel steamer was supposed to pull out of Omaha at four tomorrow morning.

Right now the boat's crew was in the process of off-loading cargo that had been brought up from St. Louis or points even more distant, and loading on more cargo destined for landings all the way up to the Great Falls beyond Benton. The river here carried all the freight that in other parts of the country would be moved by rail.

Longarm found a wharf piling with a flat top, and settled onto the thing like a stool while he smoked a cheroot and observed the process with interest.

The *Joshua C.* was only one of eight or ten boats tied up at the landing at the moment. The entire wharf district was a madhouse of activity as drays and sweating workmen labored to shift goods by the ton to and from the nearby warehouses.

Kegs, crates, and bales were stacked into miniature mountains on the wharf and on the boat decks too.

Longarm didn't see how anybody could keep all of it straight, working out what belonged to whom and how to know whether something was coming or going. And if it was going, where the hell it was going to.

Far as he could see, it was all confusion in the raw. Fortunately for the future of commerce, though, he seemed to be the only one around who didn't know exactly what was happening.

He smoked his cheroot and marveled at the busy scene in front of him, and watched as the purser came down the plank off the *Joshua C.* to set up a folding chair and an umbrella. Longarm figured that meant that passengers could board now if they wanted.

There was no rush for that, of course, particularly since there wasn't any kitchen aboard the steamer. Passengers were advised to bring their own groceries if they intended to eat anytime during the six- to eight-day journey upriver. Longarm already had his supplies bought.

Now that he thought about it and had time to look the *Joshua C.* over with a critical eye, he could see that the boat didn't offer much of anything in the way of comforts. But then it was intended as a hauler of cargo, not carefree passengers. Passenger tickets were just a little extra form of profit for the owners, he suspected.

The boat looked for the most part like a—it didn't please him a helluva lot to make the connection—huge coffin with no lid. It was just a long, squared-off wood box, blunt at both ends and with a steam engine plunked down in the middle and a paddle wheel slung on either side. Sixty feet long, he judged, or maybe more. Slab-sided wood sheds had been erected in front of the engine and behind to give some shelter to the captain and crew and to provide crude accommodations for the passengers. Longarm hadn't seen a passenger cabin yet, but he knew better than to expect much. If there was a cot to lie down on, he would figure it was enough.

Most of the boat consisted of deck space. And near every square inch of that by now was piled with cargo. To a man who was happier on the back of a horse than floating around on top of more murky river water than was needed for drinking purposes, the outfit looked like it would surely founder under all that weight and sink plumb out of sight. Longarm rather hoped he was wrong about that.

He decided he probably should treat himself to one last good meal before the boat splashed away from Omaha. It might be the last decent food he could expect until he reached Benton. Which would be all right so long as it wasn't the last decent food he could expect, period.

He carried his things over to the plank and identified himself to the purser first, figuring there was no need to drag saddle and everything with him when he went looking for supper.

"Yes, sir, Mr. Long, pleasure to have you aboard. You'll be in cabin two, immediately aft the engine, sir."

"You think you just told me where to find it, don't you?" Longarm said with a smile.

The purser laughed and this time pointed. "Behind the engine, sir. First cabin behind all that machinery you see there."

"This time I reckon I can thank you an' mean it."

"Just stow your gear under the bunks, sir. Sorry, but we don't have anyone to help you with it."

"No need. I reckon I can manage by myself." He carried his things through the narrow aisles left between the piles of cargo and found the cabin.

It was worse—make that smaller—than he had feared. The so-called cabin was big enough to make a fair broom closet. And it held four bunks racked double deep on both sides with just enough room between them for a thin man to squeeze through. The bunks were six feet long—some inches shorter than Longarm's height—and were nailed nice and secure to the front and back walls of the cabin space.

If all those bunks were to be used, this was going to be an interesting trip. It was a good thing Longarm hadn't expected much in the way of luxury.

He deposited his things on the floor and gave a shove with his foot to send it all sliding underneath the bunk on his right, then turned and got the hell out of there.

The next trick would be wobbling across that gangplank again on these high boot heels. He was damn sure going to have to come back to the boat sober tonight, or he'd be swimming for sure.

A good meal, though. A drink or two. Maybe a friendly game of cards to pass some of the time between sundown and departure. Hell, it was going to work out all right.

Chapter 4

Hell. Now Longarm wished he had come back to the boat drunk.

Too drunk, anyhow, to keep his sense of smell.

The cabin he walked into was also being occupied by another traveler. Just one, thank goodness, but this particular one was more than enough.

The man—Longarm couldn't see his face for the blanket that was dragged up over it—was snoring louder than most steam whistles.

Longarm could put up with a man's snoring if he had to. Hell, that wasn't the guy's fault, after all. It wasn't like it was something done a'purpose to annoy.

But this man had gas enough to light a fair-sized city.

Longarm's cabin mate for the voyage smelled like a skunk had crawled up his ass and died there. Last month.

"Oh, shit," Longarm mumbled. He backed out of the cabin and gulped in deep breaths of fresh air gratefully. "Oh, shit," he repeated, louder this time.

Whatever that other river traveler had had for supper, Longarm hoped he never ran into any of the stuff. It must've been lethal to cause this.

He eyed the cabin door, and regretted that it couldn't be pulled open and left that way. The problem was that there was so little clearance between the cabin wall and the cargo piled on the deck nearby that no one could get through if the door was left ajar. And there wasn't a window to leave open through the night.

If that poor SOB in there had himself a chronic problem with farting, this trip was going to be an exercise in agony. Maybe his own. Longarm was already beginning to wonder what the captain did if a passenger turned up missing overboard. Not that that'd work if it delayed the trip. Dammit.

Longarm wrinkled his nose and wormed his way between stacks of baled soft goods—tarpaulins? blankets? tents?— to a pile of crates at the back of the boat.

He was tired, but not so much so that he wanted to go back inside that cabin again.

It was one, two o'clock in the morning, he judged, and the crew of the *Joshua C.* was either sleeping or ashore for one last fling. Longarm hadn't seen or heard another waking soul since he left the tavern where he'd just won a couple dollars five and ten cents at a time.

The boat was scheduled to leave at four, so there was plenty of time yet for the captain and crew to get around to doing whatever it was they did.

The night air back here was fresh, the breeze sweeping down the Missouri and carrying away the city smells of coal smoke and the wharf smells of tar and dead fish. Any of those, though, would have been preferable to the smells waiting in Longarm's cabin.

As it was, he particularly enjoyed the freshness in the air and the sight of the stars overhead. He found a crate to perch on, and pulled a cheroot out of his pocket.

If it came to that, he decided, he could sleep on top of one of those bales for as long as the weather held.

He took his time trimming the end off the cheroot, then rolled it on his tongue to moisten the pale wrapper leaf. He

19

fished into a pocket in search of a match.

"Ma'am." The voice, low and polite, came from somewhere to his right.

"Sir?" The answer was a woman's voice.

"Didn't mean t' disturb you, ma'am. Didn't know there was anybody back here."

"That is quite all right, sir. I was too excited to get to sleep. I walked out to look at the stars, you see. They're so pretty."

"Yes, ma'am."

Longarm felt a trifle uncomfortable to find himself eavesdropping on someone else's conversation, innocent though it was. He held the match instead of lighting it. His smoke could wait a moment.

"A pretty young thing like you oughta be careful, ma'am. Bein' out here alone like this an' nobody around. You shoulda brung your travelin' companion with you."

The woman's voice chuckled softly. "But I am traveling alone, you see."

"Do tell." The man's voice sounded interested. And less polite now.

"Yes. I am traveling all the way up into Montana Territory. Do you know it?"

"Can't say as I do."

"My fiancé is there. It is newly opened country. Full of opportunity, I am told. You haven't heard of it?"

"What I know, little lady, is that you're mighty likely-lookin'. Nice tits I see under that robe there."

Longarm frowned. He could hear the woman's voice gasp.

"Really, sir, I—"

"You here travelin' all alone like this. No man fer a thousand miles. Come out in public in your nightclothes, flashin' your tits. Makes a man kinda think, it does."

"Sir! Please."

Longarm was already moving, even before he heard the scraping of feet on wood and the subdued sounds of a struggle.

He jumped down onto the deck, found his way along the

20

stern blocked by the piled cargo, and began scrambling over the top of the crates.

"Hel—" The shout for help was cut short.

The man's voice laughed, the sound of it nasty in the darkness. "Just you hol' still there, girly, an' we'll have us some fun. Hol' *still*, I said."

Longarm reached the top of the stack of crates and came onto all fours. Not in this aisle. The space below him was dark and empty, the muffled sounds of continuing struggle coming from beyond the next pile of cargo. He heard a near-silent squeal and a thump, and a sound that might have been cloth being roughly torn.

He came to his feet, paused for a split second to get his balance, and leaped across the narrow aisle from one cargo pile to the next.

A keg there shifted. He lost his balance, and had to drop to hands and knees again to keep from falling.

"Tha's nice, girly. Jus' you hol' still. Jus' like that. Gimme a minute here t' get this thing out where we can enjoy it, see. No, now don't you try an' bite me, you li'l bitch, or I'll have to go an' hurt you. Hol' still an' I won't hurt you none. It'll be a pleasure. You'll see."

Longarm threw himself across the wobbly kegs.

The man and the struggling, frantic young woman were immediately below him.

The man, a thick-bodied, burly son of a bitch, had a hand clamped hard over the woman's mouth. His other hand was fumbling at his own fly. He had already yanked the front of her robe open, and the remains of her nightdress were in tatters, exposing her body pale in the starlight.

The man chuckled and started to reach for the woman's crotch once he had his pecker free.

Longarm dropped to the deck behind the SOB.

He would have planted his boot heels on the back of the bastard's neck except that might have hurt the woman too.

"What th' . . . " He tried to turn and found himself turning into Longarm's flashing fist.

Bone and gristle shattered with a loud pop, and blood splattered to both sides as the rapist's nose was pulped.

21

The man tried to kick Longarm in retaliation. Longarm grabbed his ankle and pulled, spilling the rapist onto his back in the narrow aisle.

The man squirmed, trying to kick free and to haul himself back away from this unexpected assault.

Longarm held onto his leg, warded off a kick by the bastard's free foot, and lifted his own boot heel high.

The rapist was lying on his back with his trousers at half mast and his privates exposed.

The target of opportunity seemed entirely appropriate under the circumstances. Longarm smashed down hard, the narrow heel of the stockman's boot crushing the rapist's balls.

The man screamed louder than any woman ever could have. He was reaching for a pitch as high as a woman's too.

"Sorry, ma'am," Longarm said.

The would-be rapist didn't seem much interested in fighting anymore. He was crying and holding himself and rolling back and forth in agony, knocking against first one wall of crates and then over against the pile of kegs. He was trying to wriggle away at the same time, and was bumping up against the young woman's feet.

"Let me help you, miss." Longarm reached across the supine body of the unhappy rapist and helped the girl over the obstruction.

She seemed in a state of mild shock after the fury of the attempted rape and then the unexpected violence of the rescue. She stood with her hands to her throat, staring down at the man who had just tried to violate her.

Longarm took her by the shoulders and turned her away so she couldn't see, then reached down and pulled the folds of her robe closed to cover the nakedness that she seemed for the moment to have forgotten.

He smiled and softly told her, "It's all right now, ma'am. You're safe."

He could hear footsteps approaching from the front of the boat. He checked again to see that she was covered. The robe had begun to gape open again, so he pulled it

22

into position once more and refastened the cloth belt to hold it more firmly closed. He tried to ignore the fact that the rapist had been right about the quality of the young woman's breasts. "Everything is all right now," he told her gently.

Two people he recognized as crewmen on the *Joshua C.* reached them, both men armed with wicked-looking short clubs.

"Whoa, boys. Easy now. The fella you want is that one on the floor there. The lady's all right. He attacked her, but I happened t' overhear."

The nearer crewman gave Longarm a suspicious look, then turned to the woman. "Is that right, Miss Day?"

She nodded and bit at her underlip.

"Louie, take Miss Day to her cabin. This gentleman and me'll see to cleaning up the garbage here."

"Right. This way, ma'am. You're all right now."

Everybody, himself no exception, was telling the girl, whose name seemed to be Day, that she was all right. Longarm hoped that was so. She had suffered the trauma of the attack even if the rape had not been completed.

The crew member called Louie led her away. The other man waited until Miss Day was out of sight before he turned and leaned down over the still-thoroughly-miserable rapist.

The crewman was not a particularly large or powerful-looking man, but he picked the moaning rapist up without apparent effort and held him off the deck, looking him over the way someone might inspect a rat removed alive from a spring trap. He exposed his teeth at the rapist, but Longarm didn't think anyone who saw it would call the expression a smile.

Then the crewman turned to Longarm and in an unexpectedly polite tone said, "You can go back to bed now, Mr. Long. We'll take care of this problem."

Longarm considered identifying himself as a deputy marshal, then thought better of it. Better if he didn't start that yet. There was no telling how far the information might spread if it once got started. He settled for saying, "Won't the police want to take a statement from me?"

"Oh, I wouldn't know about that, sir. I expect if they want to talk to you, they can ask."

"However the captain wants to handle it will be fine with me," Longarm said.

"Yes, sir. Thank you, sir. And if the captain or the police need you, sir, we'll know where to find you."

"Fine." He had no idea what had happened to the cheroot he'd been about to light. He pulled another one out and lighted it.

"Please go back to your cabin now, Mr. Long. We'll be getting real busy on deck here in a little while, and we wouldn't want you to get bumped around."

Longarm gave the crewman a skeptical look, but decided to leave the man to his work.

He still didn't want to go back to the cabin with its foul odors, so he settled for going forward to the front of the boat, where he could enjoy his smoke in peace.

Within a half hour the *Joshua C.* was abuzz with activity as the steam engine began to hiss and chatter. By Longarm's watch the boat pulled away from the Omaha wharf precisely on time.

And he never was visited by either the local police or the boat's captain to question him about the attempted rape.

He thought that over while the sidewheeler splashed and churned its way against the slow, powerful current of the great river.

Better, he decided, to leave it be, at least for the time being.

After all, neither murder nor vigilante justice fell under federal jurisdiction.

And he couldn't work up a whole hell of a lot of sympathy for that rapist, no matter what had happened to the son of a bitch.

Longarm smoked another cheroot, leaned back against a bale of yard goods, and dozed until the bright light of dawn roused him.

Chapter 5

River travel on a boat intended for the transport of cargo was basically a boring proposition. Passengers were something to be tolerated and kept out of the way, and no provision had been made for their comfort, much less their pleasure.

Even so, this was the fastest way to where he had to go, so Longarm figured he could put up with it.

He waited on the forward deck until well past dawn, then threaded his way through the cargo stacks and past the groaning, clanking steam engine to the cabin he'd been assigned.

His cabin mate was still asleep. Although how anyone could sleep through the racket made by the engine was entirely beyond Longarm's comprehension.

At least now the man had quit passing wind. The cabin smelled stale, but no worse than that. Longarm dragged out his sack of provisions and got a couple of cold biscuits and a hunk of jerked meat to breakfast on, then carried them outside to the cleaner air on deck.

He very nearly bumped into the young woman he had seen but not actually met last night.

"Ma'am." He touched his hat brim and squeezed back against a pile of crates so she could get by. She didn't take advantage of the opportunity, though. She looked at him and blushed.

"I owe you my thanks."

"No thanks necessary, Miss Day. I was glad to be of help."

She was still blushing. He could imagine why. He'd seen her as good as naked last night after the would-be rapist ripped her nightdress apart.

In daylight, Longarm could despise the man's actions but couldn't find much fault with his judgment. Miss Day truly was an attractive young woman.

Eighteen or nineteen, he suspected, with red highlights in her light brown hair and large, luminous green eyes. Irish ancestry, perhaps? She had the peaches-and-cream complexion for it.

Her face was heart-shaped and delicate, her lips pale but quite full and nicely shaped.

As for nice shapes, well, her figure, as Longarm knew uncomfortably well, was better than merely good. Her waist was small and her hips nicely rounded. And her tits were monumental.

Poets should write sonnets commemorating tits like those. Songs should be sung to them and artworks sculpted.

Miss Day acted now like she hadn't an idea in the world about what effect her full-figured good looks would have on any male above the age of puberty and not yet more than two days in the grave.

She blushed and kept her eyes down away from Longarm's.

"We haven't been properly introduced," she said.

"No, ma'am, and I'm afraid it wouldn't really be possible under these circumstances. May I introduce myself? Custis Long, ma'am. At your service." He removed his hat and tried to sweep it gallantly into a bow. The effect was diminished somewhat because there wasn't room enough in

26

the passageway for him to complete the gesture. He barked his knuckles rather painfully on the side of a crate when he tried it.

If Miss Day saw, she didn't give any sign of it. "I am Miss Loretta Day, sir, of Louisville, Kentucky. Affianced to Mr. Andrew Moresbeck, recently of Montana."

"My pleasure, Miss Day."

"Thank you, I . . . could you advise me, Mr. Long?"

"Certainly."

"I don't know where the dining room is on this boat, you see . . ."

Longarm frowned. "There isn't one, miss."

"No?" She looked up for the first time, a hint of panic in her pretty eyes. "But I thought . . . why, I was sure, sir . . ."

"I'm sorry, miss. Passengers on these cargo boats are supposed to carry their own provisions."

"Oh, dear!" Her hand came up to her throat, and she looked like she might be about to cry.

Longarm felt a quick pang of sympathy for her. Last night she'd told that rapist, before she realized what he was up to and when she was trying to be friendly, that she was traveling alone to meet her husband-to-be.

"Look, uh, would it help if I shared my stuff with you, Miss Day? It isn't much. Sure isn't fancy. But it'd keep body and soul together until we get to the next landing. I'd be glad to share it with you."

"I've already imposed on you so much, Mr. Long," she protested.

"Not at all," he insisted. "Here."

He held out the biscuits and jerky he'd intended for his own breakfast. Miss Day eyed them like she thought they might have bugs on them, then daintily accepted them with another blush. "You are very kind, sir."

"My pleasure, miss."

"If there is any way I can repay you, Mr. Long . . ."

"No need for that," he assured her.

Which was a bit of a lie but only a small one. There *was* a way, of course.

27

Longarm winced at the thought. But damn, she was a fine-looking female.

And those magnificent tits.

He just damn well couldn't help but think about it.

Sliding under the sheets with one like that . . . shee-it. The thought was enough to give a monk a hard-on.

He suspected Miss Day's presence aboard the *Joshua C.* all the way to Montana was going to make his nights plenty uncomfortable. And those of every other man on board too.

Look-but-don't-touch was not a game grown men liked to play.

Still and all, that was a game that a man sometimes just had to accept, like it or don't.

And it wasn't like any of it was Miss Day's fault. She couldn't help the way she looked. Didn't seem to even know the effect she had when her eyelashes fluttered. Sure didn't seem to understand the discomfort her blushes might cause. Hell, a girl like that wouldn't know anything about a man's urges. Probably had no notion what a man was built like, much less had she ever seen an erect and eager cock.

You could tell just by looking at her that this young and innocent girl was virginal in mind as well as in body.

But damn, he wished she would learn to wear a loose-fitting duster when she was traveling instead of a gown belted tight at the waist and cut close around her hips.

There wasn't any way, of course, she could hide those tits.

A bull-hide breast band couldn't strap those things down. Not with three men and a boy straining to cinch it tight.

Shee-oot.

"Thank you for your kindness, Mr. Long. Again." She smiled and prettily blushed. "If there is ever anything I can do . . . "

"Please don't think about it again, miss." He touched the brim of his Stetson and watched appreciatively as Miss Day carried his breakfast, now hers, back to the privacy of her cabin.

Longarm rolled his eyes and went back to his own quarters for a replacement meal.

28

Chapter 6

It had taken eight and a half days for the *Joshua C.* to reach Fort Benton, and Longarm was quite frankly pleased to hear that the landing would be reached within the hour.

He and the other passengers were seated, as had become usual, on a section of the forward deck where cargo had been cleared away by deliveries made early in the voyage.

Miss Loretta Day was, as had become usual, seated next to him.

The girl, innocent and wide-eyed as she was, had become something of a nuisance over the days past.

She seemed to have adopted Longarm as her protector and confidant. And also as her supplier of food, beverages, advice, companionship . . . whatever she required. Somehow it had become a habit.

It wasn't a particularly comfortable one.

Pretty as she was, and since she was the only female on the boat, Longarm was getting just plain horny from being near her almost every waking hour.

He didn't really resent sharing his food with her. But he was becoming more than a bit annoyed by the fact that at this point she no longer seemed especially appreciative of his help. She was accepting it all by now as quite a matter of course.

The few other passengers were just as horny, he suspected—for the past several nights he thought he'd overheard his cabin mate, Barnly, pulling his pud in the small hours—but at least they didn't have to be with the girl all day every day.

Longarm wouldn't have thought it possible when he started out on the muddy river, but today he was going to be damned glad to be shut of the young and undeniably lovely Miss Loretta Day as a traveling companion. She was staying with the steamer all the way to the Great Falls.

"I shall be sure to tell my fiancé Mr. Moresbeck of your kindness, Mr. Long," she assured him now with one of those mood-melting, pecker-erecting smiles of hers.

Longarm gritted his teeth and tried to smile back at her. "My fiancé Mr. Moresbeck." Fifty times a day he'd heard that phrase. He was more than a little sick of it. It was never just "my fiancé" or just "Mr. Moresbeck," certainly never Andrew, nor, heaven forbid, Andy. It was every time the whole string, "my fiancé Mr. Moresbeck." Longarm was beginning to wonder if she'd ever met the poor son of a bitch. Not that he wanted to prolong a conversation by asking. He managed a smile somehow and reached for a cheroot. She never seemed to mind the smoke. But he kept hoping.

From the corner of his eye as he bent over the match flame he couldn't help but see those marvelous, magnificent, mountainous tits poking his way from under a thin shirtwaist. Dammit.

A man could grab hold of those handles and . . . Never mind that sort of thinking, he reminded himself. The boat wasn't to Benton yet.

Over on the far side of the impromptu passenger area he could see Barnly and the seedy gambler who called himself

Harris whispering and snickering. He could guess what they were saying. He only wished that all of it were true. Or any of it.

The simple fact was that Miss Day was as virginal now as the moment she'd walked aboard this creaky excuse for a sidewheeler. Longarm hadn't so much as touched her wrist. Hell, she'd have been shocked if he did. And more's the pity for it.

Miss Day waited for him to get his smoke drawing nicely, then leaned so close that he could feel—or imagine that he felt—the warmth seeping off her nipples. "Could I ask you something, Mr. Long? In strictest confidence, of course. It is something . . . I mean . . . I don't wish to be indelicate . . . but I have no female acquaintances to discuss this with, and . . . "

She blushed. Longarm wouldn't have thought it possible for a man to be annoyed by the sight of a pretty girl blushing. It was possible.

"Of course, Miss Day." Another hour. Less. He could put up with anything that long. He smiled at her.

Her blush became even deeper and her whispering even more hesitant. She leaned so close that this time he could feel the press of her flesh, that particular flesh, against the side of his arm. She reached upward so that he could feel the warmth of her breath in his ear. Damn it.

"When I reach my destination, Mr. Long, and, um, my fiancé Mr. Moresbeck and I are, uh, united in matrimony . . . ?"

She seemed unable to get the rest of her question out. "Yes, Miss Day?"

"I was wondering, sir—in your opinion, that is—is it not possible for a gentleman and a lady to be, to have, that is, a marital . . . relationship that is . . . that would be . . . platonic?" The blushing in her cheeks threatened to set her hair afire by now.

"God, no," Longarm blurted out.

"Oh!" She sat back, her lovely eyes even wider now in shock. "Oh, dear."

"Look, I, uh, I'm sorry. I think maybe I'm the wrong

31

guy for you to ask that. I mean, it isn't like I know your Mr. Moresbeck. Right?"

"I see what you mean. Yes. Thank you." She kept her eyes down for a moment, then perked up and smiled again. "I shall cope, Mr. Long. I just know I shall."

"Yeah, I'm sure you'll do that, Miss Day. Look, would you excuse me now? I think we're coming to the landing, and I have to get my things together." He was already long since packed and ready, of course. His gear lay on top of his bunk, and needed only to be carried down the plank when he left the boat at Benton.

"Of course, Mr. Long." She held a gloved hand up so he could touch her fingertips. "I have truly enjoyed your company on my trip, Mr. Long. You shall never know how much. Thank you."

He shivered. "Yeah, well, me too, Miss Day." He smiled and bowed and got the hell back to the safety of privacy in the tiny cabin.

It had been a disquieting river voyage indeed, and he was grateful when he felt the front—bow, the rivermen called it—of the boat begin to swing toward the landing at Fort Benton. The *Joshua C.* would be there several hours unloading cargo and taking on wood for the boiler, but Longarm figured to be on solid ground again within two seconds of that gangplank touching the landing.

Chapter 7

Longarm felt positively free as he walked the stretch of rutted, hard-packed dirt that served as a street in the little civilian community that had grown up near the army post at Fort Benton.

It was easy enough to replenish his supplies of food, cheroots, and whiskey in the town, but finding a horse proved to be a more difficult matter.

There were none to rent, and only three for sale that he could discover. And the best of those would only be suited to slicing and frying.

"Wish I could help you, mister, but I cain't. Dang Remount Service is slow t' ship stock all this way north, so th' army boys mostly buy up anything decent that comes available hereabouts. They're s' needful of fresh horses that the band is ridin' grays an' pintos."

That was serious, all right. Officially the army would only accept browns, blacks, and bays for government service, Longarm knew. Once in a great while a unit might be mounted uniformly on grays. But paints and pintos were taboo. Obviously the Justice Department was not the only branch of government that was inconvenienced by the slowness of transportation and communication this far north.

"I need something to ride," Longarm said, offering the man a smoke, "and none of these will do."

"Cain't say as I blame you." The fellow, who dealt more in wood for the riverboats than in livestock judging by the state of his yard, accepted the cheroot. "Got one other possibility you might could try, friend."

"I'd appreciate the suggestion."

"There's an outfit in the brakes downriver from here eight, ten mile. Fella lived there used t' cut wood for me an' had him a start on a horse-raisin' business. Was just cuttin' wood, see, till he could get his herd producin' cash money. Don't know if there's anything left there t' sell, but I 'spect his widow woman would be grateful for the income if she has anything left."

"Widow?"

"Aye. Fella slipped in the snow last winter when he was cuttin', an' a tree come down smack atop him. Mussed up his insides. Hung on a few days an' died. Don't know what's become o' things since then, y' understand."

"It's worth a try," Longarm agreed. "You say it's eight or ten miles down?"

"Uh, huh. Got a cart here an' miniature mule t' pull it. Rig ain't pretty, but it'd get you there an' back. I'd rent it t' you for a dollar."

"Fair enough."

It was late afternoon by the time Longarm reached the wagon path cut into the thick growth along the Missouri. It was the fourth turning he had come to, and was marked with a shattered wagon tongue stuck upright in the ground, so it pretty much had to be the place the livery man had told him about.

"Gee, Ulysses, gee up there, boy." The little mule responded as readily to "gee" and "haw" voice commands as it did to the lines. It flicked its ears and obediently turned

34

to the right, guiding itself onto the path without Longarm having to touch the reins that he'd long since tied to the empty whip socket.

The light cart rattled and bumped through the brush until the makeshift road dead-ended in a riverbank clearing.

Longarm sighed. If indeed this was the place that was supposed to have horses to sell, he might be going away disappointed again. There was a solidly built low cabin, but no outbuildings or corrals anywhere in sight.

"Whoa, Ulysses, whoa." The mule came to an abrupt halt and waited patiently for its next command.

Longarm climbed down off the cart and stretched.

"Hello?" There was a woman's face peering hesitantly out from a partially opened cabin door.

"Ma'am." Longarm removed his hat and tried to look inoffensive. "I was told in town that you might have a horse to sell?"

"Who are you?" She sounded suspicious.

"Name's Custis Long, ma'am. Come about a horse. Nothing else."

She sniffed. "I have a gun, you know."

"Yes, ma'am, and so you should."

"You want to buy a horse or borrow one?"

"Buy, ma'am."

"Cash money?"

"Yes, ma'am." She brightened considerably after that. The door swung the rest of the way open and she came outside, no sign of any kind of weapon on her.

The lady of the house was a scrawny, work-worn little woman whose dress had seen too many washings and too many repairs. She was barefoot, and her hair was held back in a twist of cloth instead of with pins. She looked like the prospect of some cash in hand would be better than merely welcome. Longarm had no idea how old she might be. She had the sun-dried, wrinkled look that hard work can give a woman in her twenties, but she as easily could have been forty. He couldn't help an uncharitable comparison between this woman and fresh, dewy Miss Loretta Day. If this little woman had any tits, he couldn't spot them under her apron.

35

"You sure you got cash, mister?"

"Yes, ma'am." He guessed that hard money was a rarity around here. "You do have horses to sell, you say?"

"Didn't say, but my man left me some geldings along with the brood stock and some young fillies. He's dead, you know." Longarm assumed she was talking about the husband, not any horses. "They aren't broke very good. Haven't been messed with since my man died."

"He'd got them started, though?"

"Last summer, he did. They were two then. Three now. Green broke but decent built. I'll show you."

Three was younger than Longarm liked to see in a using horse, but it would be enough if the knee joints were fully developed. Generally speaking he disapproved of starting a horse under saddle at two. But he was willing to accept the exception this time, particularly if it meant the difference between riding to Beck City, Montana, or following Ulysses' furry ears all that way.

"Thank you, ma'am."

He trailed her around to the side of the cabin and onto a footpath hacked out of the brush there. A hundred yards of walking brought them to another clearing, this one verging on a grassy clearing that opened out to the rolling hills to the north. The clearing held a large corral, a round breaking pen, and a small shed. The corral contained a good dozen mares and as many more young horses ranging in age from sucklings to three-year-olds.

"That's the stud horse you can see grazing on the hill up there," the woman said, pointing. "I turn him out to graze in the afternoons. The mares and young'uns are let out mornings. Keep the stud in the pen otherwise."

Longarm nodded. He'd wondered about the absence of a stallion on a breeding outfit.

"The geldings you might be interested in would be that sorrel over there on the left and the little roan over there."

Longarm leaned on the top rail of the corral and spent a few moments looking the horses over. The sorrel was the leggier of the two, much the taller and prettier. But the stocky blue roan was the better built of the pair, and being smaller, was the more likely to be fully developed at that age. "I'd like to see the roan," he said.

The woman grunted. He couldn't decide if that meant approval of his choice or otherwise. She bent and started to crawl between the rails to go fetch the horse for him.

"I can do that, ma'am."

"No need, mister. He knows me. But I thank you for the offer. Been a long time since I've been treated like a lady." As soon as she was inside the corral the horses began moving toward her. "Toss me that rope there, please."

He did. She slipped it loosely around the roan's neck and led it to the gate, then over to the breaking pen so he could examine it more closely.

"This one will do me fine," he said after a bit.

"Twenty . . . " She hesitated, then added, "Five dollars?"

A green broken horse this age was probably worth fifteen. He nodded. "Twenty-five sounds fair," he said. After all, it was coming out of the Attorney General's budget, not the marshal's.

She smiled, and couldn't suppress a sigh of relief. Twenty-five dollars in cash carefully held and sparingly used might carry her in salt and flour for another year.

"Do you have a saddle with you?"

"Yes, ma'am."

"If you don't want to carry it through, you can go back out and drive around. I'd suggest you spend some time in the round pen reminding him of his manners before you trust him very far. Time you do that, mister, I'll have supper on the table."

"Thank you, ma'am."

Longarm knew better than to refuse the offer. No matter how little she had to share with a stranger, she would be insulted if he rejected the hospitality.

On the other hand, there was no good reason why he shouldn't spend a little time looking for a fat whitetail to knock down and hang under the eaves for her. Getting the

37

roan reacquainted with a saddle shouldn't take so long that he would have to forget his side of the manners.

"I'll expect you before dark," she said.

"Yes, ma'am, I'll look forward to that." He walked with her back to the cabin to collect his saddle.

Chapter 8

Longarm yawned and stretched his toes underneath the blanket. He'd laid his bedroll out on the riverbank behind the cabin and was content enough now.

He could have ridden back to Benton in the dark, but really didn't want to trust the young roan at night. Not until he got to know the horse better. Young animals saw boogers even in broad daylight, and shadows could be frightening to them. Better not to let a bad habit get started if it could be avoided to begin with.

The roan promised to be a better-than-average animal once its education was completed. As it was right now, it should be entirely usable.

The lady had had supper ready by the time Longarm was done reminding the roan of its purpose, and had invited him inside so he could eat. And so he could pay her the twenty-five dollars in hard money too, of course.

Supper had been catfish drenched in cornmeal and deep fried, and there had been no shortage of the tasty fish to fill up on. The cornmeal had been in scantier supply, he saw, but the woman had done her best to set a full table for her guest.

Instead of coffee she'd brewed an herb tea of some sort, which he had insisted on replacing with coffee beans from his own supplies. He could stock up again in Benton before he pulled south in the morning.

Now he settled in under the blankets with the soft, slow sounds of the river in his ears and the shelter of trees overhead.

Sleep came quickly and pleasantly.

He hadn't been asleep very long, though, before footsteps in the night roused him again. He sat up with the big Colt in his hand.

A moving shadow came forward without pause. Whoever it was hadn't seen that he was awake and armed.

Longarm's eyes darted and shifted, never staring directly at the half-seen figure but flickering all around it.

The person was small, he could see.

It was the woman. A sliver of moonlight streaming through the canopy of foliage showed him that.

Even so, Longarm did not let his guard down. A woman could pull a trigger as readily as a man, and it was not impossible that she'd been having thoughts about the money that might remain in her guest's pockets.

He lay where he was and let her come closer.

His bed was on a soft, grassy flat beside the slope of the river bank.

She came to the edge of the brush and stopped there.

Longarm could see no weapons. He thought her hands were empty. He wasn't going to stake his life on that as a fact, though.

She stood there for what seemed a long time, although it couldn't have been more than three or four minutes actually.

Trying to work up her nerve to shoot him? Or something else?

She took one hesitant step forward. Then another.

The moonlight bathed her again, and Longarm could see that she was not armed.

She still wore the drab, shapeless dress, but had removed her apron. Her hair hung loose and full, falling well below her shoulders. It looked freshly brushed. The change made her appear at least a little younger.

Longarm pretended to be asleep as she came nearer and stood over him, looking down at him in his blankets.

She was close enough that Longarm could hear her breathe. She seemed nervous. Yet there still was no glint of metal to indicate that she might be armed with anything more deadly than her own teeth. Longarm figured he just might be able to take her should she jump him barehanded. He doubted she weighed ninety pounds.

She'd been working up her nerve, he saw after a few minutes more.

But not to jump him.

She sobbed softly in the night and yanked the hem of her dress up over her head.

The sudden, unexpected motion startled him.

She held the dress out at arm's length and dropped it onto the grass.

She hadn't been wearing anything else.

Her body was pale in the moonlight and very small. Even in light this poor he could see the ladder of bone that was her ribcage. Her thighs were so small he could have put his hands around them fingertip to fingertip, and her breasts were meager little saucers of flesh mounted on a chest as hard and bony as a Cheyenne warrior's willow breastplate. The patch of hair at her vee was inky black in the poor light.

Even now, having made up her mind and come to him naked and needing, she hesitated a moment longer.

It occurred to Longarm that it wasn't screwing that she needed from him. It would be closeness with another human that she was hungry for.

She needed to be held and hugged and pressed warm and secure against another body.

She didn't really need sex. She needed comforting. She was willing to give the one in order to get the other.

41

He took his hand off the Colt. It wouldn't be that that he needed tonight.

She knelt at the side of his blankets, paused a moment more, then lifted the edge of the rough woolen cloth and slipped beneath it at his side.

He thought she was weeping softly as she came to him.

"Mister?" she whispered. "Mister Long? Don't be scared by me waking you. I don't mean you harm."

Nor did he mean her any harm.

He reached up and gently touched her cheek. Stroked her hair and pulled her close against him.

She sighed and buried her face against his throat.

He could feel the trembling in her frail body, and he whispered softly to her, meaningless phrases meant only to soothe, and held her close, giving her the warmth and the comfort that she needed that night.

Chapter 9

She was trembling again. But for a different reason this time. Just as the rhythm of her breathing had changed. It had been frightened and hurting. Now it was eager as her body made its own responses, as one need was met and another came to the surface.

Longarm had been stroking and gentling and soothing her for three-quarters of an hour or more. Now he could feel the changes as her thin body lost tension and seemed to melt against him.

He quit stroking the bony planes of her back and pressed her flat against the blanket.

He ran the tip of his tongue over her eyelids and inside the curve of her ear, then down her jaw and onto her lips.

She kissed him. Her breath was sweet to the taste and her lips mobile.

He pressed his palm flat against her belly and lightly moved it upward to her breasts. They didn't seem so meager now. Her nipples were tiny, hard buttons of erect flesh. He touched and teased and played with them, and her hips moved in silent response.

She gasped and reached between them to find his fly and unfasten the buttons there.

Longarm's hand slid down across soft, satiny flesh, encountering the curly brush of hair there and dipped between her thighs. She sighed as she opened herself to him.

He explored the damp, warm opening, then ran a fingertip up through the fold of flesh to the other, even smaller erect button of her pleasure.

She cried out at his touch and raised herself to him.

He kissed her again and rubbed the ball of his thumb across the hypersensitive nubbin.

Her hips pumped, and she grasped him with her skinny thighs.

He slipped a finger inside and then another, still rubbing gently at the clitoris.

A low, keening moan started deep in her throat, and her head arched backward.

She shuddered, her flesh pulsing and clenching at him as she reached an impossibly quick climax from that simple fondling.

Longarm smiled and withdrew for a moment so she could rest and recuperate.

"Wow," she whispered.

"Mm, hmm."

She laughed and hugged him, nuzzling the side of his neck with contentment now. She let out a long, slow, satisfied breath and then shifted her body, moving closer, placing herself half underneath him.

He kissed her, then pulled away long enough to shuck his clothing and return to her.

She was small, but no longer seemed at all bony or scrawny or undesirable.

Her skin was warm and soft against his and her mouth gentle, in no hurry this time.

He cupped her ass in his hand and pulled her tight against

him. He could feel her pubic hair against his cock. She raised her leg and hooked it over his waist and wriggled somehow even closer.

"Not quite yet," he said. "I'm in no hurry."

He fingered her again, slow and deep this time. She was wet and receptive.

Again he found her clitoris. Her response this second time was even quicker than the first had been.

She shuddered and bucked, her hips pumping in involuntary reaction to his touch, and after little more than scant seconds she came, her breath whistling in and out through tightly clenched teeth.

She cried out loud in the darkness, and somewhere nearby unseen wings beat against the air as a night bird was startled into flight.

Longarm chuckled and kissed her. He patted her hip and stroked her breasts.

She sighed and reached down to wrap her fingers warm around him.

"So nice," she said.

"Thank you."

"All of you, that is. Not just this. But this is awful nice too." He could feel her smile against his lips.

"Glad you approve."

She sighed again.

She ran both hands up and down his shaft. Leaned lower so she could heft and warm his balls. "If my stallion had equipment this nice . . . "

He laughed.

She ducked underneath the blanket and licked his chest. Then down onto his belly.

"Now that you went and started it," he said, "I hope you aren't just teasing."

"Oh, I mean it, all right." She laughed too. And moved lower.

He couldn't see what she was doing. But he could feel it plenty well.

Moist heat enveloped him. She tongued the head, then drew it slowly into her mouth. Longarm stroked her hair

45

and back as she lowered herself onto him, taking more of his shaft into herself.

She hesitated there for a moment, giving herself time to accommodate his size.

He could feel her slim body grow tense, and her jaw opened wider. He thought she was going to gag and pull back, but she didn't. After a few seconds she conquered the reflex and pressed down again.

There was a moment of resistance, then he felt the wet, welcome heat along the full length of his shaft, and the point of her chin dug sharply into his lower belly while she continued to cup his balls in both palms.

This was containment as complete as it was possible to get, and he closed his eyes and concentrated on enjoying the sensations she was giving him.

She began rocking back and forth, her whole body moving over and around him.

He could feel the rising surge gather and grow deep in his groin, and warned her.

She nodded, but didn't withdraw.

Longarm grunted and gave in to the pleasure of it. He sure as hell wasn't going to offer any objections.

And later there would be time enough and more to try all the other things in the ways that the two of them would share.

For now this was fine. Just fine.

He felt the long, wonderful flow begin, and she pushed tighter and harder against him, staying with him and not pulling back a fraction of an inch.

Longarm groaned and clenched his hands into fists.

This time it was his turn to give the night birds along the Missouri a scare.

Chapter 10

The cabin door was closed when Longarm woke in the morning, and there was no smoke curling out of the chimney. She might just have overslept after the night's exertions. Or the oversight might also be a hint that she didn't want to see him this morning, a matter of shame or embarrassment or who-knows-what.

Longarm decided not to push the issue, and quickly got his things together. He saddled the little roan and hitched the mule Ulysses to the cart. He figured that leading the mule and cart all the way back to Fort Benton would be good schooling for the green young horse. And forking the roan would definitely be more comfortable than driving the bouncy, unsprung cart.

The ride took two hours. By that time the roan had gotten over its sweaty nerves and was settling down nicely to road use. By that time also Longarm was hungry. He hadn't had any breakfast back at . . .

He stopped. Blinked. Then sent a rueful smile toward

nothing in particular and shook his head. Damned if he'd ever heard what the lady's name was. He shook his head again and booted the roan on into town.

By the time he'd eaten and topped off his supplies once again and located a ferry to take him across the river—and an interesting experience that was too, loading the unhappy gelding onto a boat for the first time—it was past noon.

This Beck City, where the robberies seemed to be centered, wasn't all that far in a straight line, but it was more than half a day's ride. It looked like he would have to spend at least one more night in the open.

Probably not as pleasant a one as last night had been, though.

With a little coaching, and perhaps some cussing too, he was able to convince the roan to take a smooth and easy road jog, and after that the miles flowed under the stocky little horse's hooves.

He stopped well before dusk, not because he was tired but because the roan was sweating again and shouldn't be overworked at this age and state of development.

There wasn't any harm done, of course. He wasn't going to reach Beck City without at least another half day's travel anyway.

He found a shallow swale where a few bullberries grew to provide as good a windbreak as a man could hope for in this grassy, treeless plain, and decided it was as good a place to stop as any and better than most.

The Judith Basin, which he was well into by now, was high, wide, and flat.

If a man stood on tiptoe in his stirrups he could see into next week or maybe a bit farther. And not a wrinkle or a feature to catch the eye between there and here.

Firewood would be a bitch to gather. The nearest woodlots that Longarm knew of were the ones he'd left back at the Missouri.

There was still plenty of dried buffalo dung to burn, of course, but that wouldn't last long now that the buffalo herds had been chopped down and shipped east for belting leather and pickled tongue and bonemeal fertilizer. Longarm hadn't seen but one band of the shaggy creatures all day, and there'd only been five lonesome-looking animals in that whole bunch. It was said that once you could ride all day and not be out of sight of buffalo. Ride half a day and still be inside the same herd as when you started in the morning. Those days were long gone now, and with farmers coming into the Judith wouldn't likely return again. That seemed something of a shame, but of course it was all a part of progress. And there was no avoiding progress whether you liked it or not.

Longarm unsaddled beside the bullberries, and was careful to keep hold of the roan. He knew better than to turn the critter loose and expect it to still be close in the morning. Give it a chance and it would go galloping off looking for the pals it had left behind at home.

He rubbed the horse down, and damn near punched it in the muzzle when it tried to lip his back pocket. It wasn't trying to be nippy, he realized after a moment. The young horse was lady-raised and thought it ought to be a pet instead of a tool. He gave in to the extent of letting it take some sweet grass off his palm. It seemed happier after that.

He both hobbled and picketed it to make sure it would be there come the dawn, and then let it gather its own groceries while he used twists of dried grass and some chunks of buffalo chip to cook a quick meal.

It still wasn't quite dark so he walked out onto the prairie and stood there in the dusk peering off toward the south.

The big question was: Was Ambrose Warren really involved in the shenanigans down there, or was it just a piss-poor political hack posing as a U.S. marshal that was the problem in the Judith?

Tomorrow, he figured.

He would find out tomorrow.

Chapter 11

Hooves pounded and dust flew. The roan squealed and tried to bolt. It tangled its feet into its own picket rope and toppled heavily onto its side.

Longarm didn't have time to go help it. He was flopped on the ground with his arms over his head, trying to protect himself from the tons of hairy meat that were pouring into the swale and charging blindly over him.

He took a kick in the left hip that spun him half around. He tried to curl into an even smaller target while he risked a peek over top of one forearm.

"Where in the hell did *they* come from?" he grumbled as another buffalo cow charged blindly through the swale, unable to see and avoid him in the dusk gloom and the swirl of rising dust. It passed within a few feet of him and narrowly avoided trampling him.

There were—he was able to count them now—only seven of the creatures. For just a moment there they'd seemed like seven hundred.

The band of panicked buffalo thundered up the other side of the swale and out onto the flat prairie beyond.

Longarm got to his feet with the intention of going to the roan and seeing that it was all right.

He was driven back onto his belly at the double-quick by a rifle shot somewhere out in front.

At least that explained why the buffalo were running. Some asshole was having himself some fun.

"Hey!" Longarm shouted. "Watch it!"

There was another gunshot. This time he heard the slug strike earth and go whining off into the distance.

That shot was followed in quick succession by two more.

The roan squealed and flopped against the restraint of the picket rope around its legs.

"I got one, Danny, I got me one." The voice was thin and far away.

"Quit, dammit!" Longarm hollered. "You're shooting into my camp."

Either his voice didn't carry or the idiot was too excited to pay attention to what he was hearing.

A rifle barked again, and again Longarm heard the slug strike and ricochet.

"Stop that before you hit my horse, damn you!" It hadn't honestly occurred to him to be concerned for his own safety. It was the roan he was worried about.

One of them fired another round. Longarm had no idea where that bullet went.

"Well damn you for a bunch of idjits anyhow."

He palmed his Colt and loosed three quick rounds into the air in the general direction of the riflemen. He didn't want to hit anyone, but he damn sure wanted them to know it wasn't buffalo they were shooting at over here. Not too many buffs he'd ever heard of shot back at hunters.

"Hey, watch what you're doing," an indignant voice yelped in the distance.

Longarm shook his head and spat. He should watch what *he* was doing? Thank you so much.

He reloaded the Thunderer and shoved it back into his holster, then ran over to the frightened roan and calmed it

51

with some gentle words and stroking. It was dark enough by now that he had to follow the picket rope by feel to get it unsnarled and let the horse back onto its feet. He had no idea what kind of fool it was that went hunting at this time of night.

He felt the roan front to back and top to bottom. It was nervous and trembling but didn't seem to have been hit anywhere, thank goodness.

He could hear the rattle and clunk of a wagon approaching as he worked.

"You damn well better have come over here to apologize," he said over his shoulder as the rig came to a stop close by. "And before you crawl down, move that outfit away another twenty, thirty yards. You've stopped inside the swing of my picket rope, and I don't want you making this horse any worse than you already have."

"Sorry," a voice said without sounding particularly contrite.

The rig did roll forward, though, pulling well away from the scope of the picket rope before it stopped again.

It wasn't a wagon, Longarm saw now, but a carriage with the top and side curtains erected. There were two men on the driving seat. And two rifles clattering around in a corner of the box where their sights could get knocked off line and their magazines dented. Sometimes Longarm thought folks ought to have to pass a test for common sense before they were allowed to buy a damn rifle. Common sense, that was all he'd ask. But then that'd be too much, wouldn't it. Half the damn population wouldn't be able to pass.

The driver wound his lines around the whip socket and jumped down without being invited. Longarm glared at him, but it was dark enough now that the idiot probably didn't see.

"Howdy," the man said cheerfully. His partner jumped down too and went back to open the door to the carriage. "Didn't mean to shoot into your camp, mister. We was having some fun with them buffalo, that's all. Never knew there was anybody over here."

"There was," Longarm said dryly.

"Yeah, well, no harm done." The man came closer, grinning, and shoved a hand forward to shake. "I'm Danny Barnes. That's my brother Lute. Sorry if we scared you." Danny seemed quite unaffected by what he'd just done. Likely too damn dumb to figure it out even if it was explained to him, Longarm decided sourly. Danny was barely into his twenties if he was that old, and Lute looked even younger.

"Say, mister," the boy went blithely on, "we're glad we run into you here. We was supposed to stay the night at a roadhouse, but I reckon we took a wrong turn someplace. You wouldn't have some grub we could buy off you, would you? We're on our way from Great Falls to this town in the Judith, see, and I guess we wasn't paying mind to where we was going."

Longarm frowned. He had supplies enough, true, but he lacked the inclination to share with these young assholes.

Then the one called Lute stepped back from the carriage door, and Longarm saw he was hooked for laying out the meal whether he wanted to or not. There was a lady stepping down out of the rig, and he couldn't hardly turn a lady away hungry. But he sure could question her judgment when it came to traveling companions.

"Ma'am," he said, taking his Stetson off and stepping closer.

"Why, Mr. Long. What a lovely surprise."

"Miss Day." He could recognize her in the darkness too now that she was closer.

"I thought you were going to Fort Benton, Mr. Long."

"And so I did, miss. On my way down here. I, uh, kinda thought you were on your way to Great Falls."

She smiled. "Yes. To meet these gentlemen. They brought the carriage there to convey me to my fiancé Mr. Moresbeck."

Longarm gritted his teeth. There it was again, that same expression he'd had to hear over and over all the way from Omaha to damn Benton. Miss Day hadn't changed a whole hell of a lot in the past couple days.

"You folks know each other?" Danny asked. Stupidly,

53

Longarm thought. That much shoulda been obvious even to Danny Barnes.

"Yes, of course, Danny. This is the Mr. Long I told you about. My protector on the river steamer. He was *such* a help the whole trip north. I simply don't know what I would have done without him."

"Why hell, mister," Danny said with a grin and another handshake. "We've heard all about how you saved Miss Loretta from that fella back in Omaha. If you're goin' to Beck City, mister, I know the boss is gonna want t' thank you proper."

Lute pushed closer and insisted on shaking Longarm's hand too. Both the Barnes boys were grinning and happy and quite unconcerned that they had damn near killed someone with their foolishness.

Longarm sighed and gave in to the inevitable. "You boys take care of your team and get the fire built up again. I'll see what I can put together for something for you to eat."

Chapter 12

It took more than half a day to reach Beck City come the next daylight. Longarm could have made the trip much quicker on his own, but Miss Day was insistent that he accompany the slow-moving carriage. The girl bubbled and beamed and told him over and over how grateful her fiancé Mr. Moresbeck would be for all the help he had given her.

Longarm couldn't help but wonder—uncharitably, to be sure—whether she was more interested in having him near or if she simply wanted another opportunity to dig into his grocery sack. Eating at his expense seemed to have become something of a habit with her.

Still, he didn't want to be impolite. He gritted his teeth and smiled and did what duty required. He drew the line, though, at tying the roan behind the carriage and riding inside it with her. After a while she mercifully quit suggesting it.

Danny and Lute Barnes were lighthearted, happy-go-lucky, mental lightweights who made the trip even longer by veering off in strange directions to look at whatever struck their eyes or their interest.

Fortunately there was damned little visible from one horizon to the next that could excite any interest. The Judith was one large, empty chunk of grass.

As they neared Beck City, though, the grassland was more and more frequently dotted with freshly plowed fields and squat, ugly sod houses.

All the farms looked raw and new, the virgin soil rich and dark with loam that had been fertilized by the buffalo herds for probably thousands of years. The soddies were all recently erected, their walls still square and sharply defined. In a few more years, even quicker than adobe deteriorates, the sod structures would begin to slump and melt under the influence of summer rains and winter snows.

By that time, though, the farmers who so hopefully built here would either have proved up on their land and been successful enough to build real houses . . . or they would have gone bust and no one would care if the grassroot-and-mud houses returned to the earth.

Whichever way that was going to go, only time would tell.

"Mr. Long? Mr. Long!"

"Yes, Miss Day?" He bumped the roan forward so he was riding beside the carriage window. Lute had taken the side curtains down for the drive today, but left the canvas top up so the lady would be shielded from the sun.

"Is that Beck City I can see up there? Where that smoke is. Do you see?"

The girl had good eyes. Longarm had to stand in his stirrups to make out what she was pointing toward. "Must be," he agreed.

"I'm so excited I can hardly abide it," she dithered. She leaned out over the door. "Can't you go any faster, Danny?"

"Not without riskin' a broke wheel. There's a road up ahead, miss. Wait'll we get to it. Then we'll spank 'em a little an' bring you in steppin' high."

"Please hurry, Danny." She gave Longarm a flashing

smile and actually, literally leaned forward in her seat in anticipation of the arrival.

Longarm let the roan drop back behind the carriage window before he shook his head. This girl was trouble. He hoped her fiancé Mr. Moresbeck put high value on a pillow-sized chest, because Miss Loretta Day would likely be a handful to have to live with.

Longarm edged the roan forward again until he was beside the driving box. "You boys don't need me tagging along anymore," he said in a voice that he hoped wouldn't carry. "And I'm sure Mr. Moresbeck won't want the distraction of a stranger butting in when he greets his lady. Tell Miss Day that I'll call on her an' have the honor of meeting her fiancé later."

"Whatever you say, mister," Lute said cheerfully.

Longarm put the steel to the young roan and squirted ahead of the carriage before Miss Day could see and have time to call him back.

He left the rig quickly behind and loped the rest of the way into Beck City on his own, passing farms on either side now.

The town seemed as new and as raw as the farmsteads they'd been passing for several hours.

Someone had gone to the trouble of laying it out in carefully planned squares with wide streets between and ample room left for alleys, but fewer than half of the staked and numbered town lots had been built on yet, and a good many of those structures were made of the same sod the farmers used.

There were a dozen or so wood-frame buildings, all but three of those being businesses on the main street. One of two really substantial structures in the whole town was a building on a downtown corner lot that had a brick first floor—and Lord knows how much trouble it had been to haul brick in—and a wooden second story.

Wording carved into the stone lintel over the doorway there proclaimed the place to be the Bank of Beck City.

Nearby there was a two-story sod building, a rarity but certainly not unheard of, with a sign out front reading "City

Hall" in large letters and "Town Marshal" in a smaller hand. There was something about a multi-story sod building that always struck Longarm as being strange, but you saw such a thing every once in a while.

Also on the main street there were assorted stores, one cafe, and two saloons, but no hotel that Longarm could see.

The busiest place in town seemed to be the smithy at the far end of the street. The blacksmith had a sod building to work in and a broad yard at the side where farm implements were drawn up waiting for repairs or possibly for sale. There was also a small corral attached to the back of the smithy, probably as close as Beck City could get to having a wagon park and livery.

Since it was somewhat easier to get information from people than from things, and since most of the people in view were concentrated at the blacksmith's, Longarm headed toward the smithy for his first stop in Beck City, Montana Territory.

The smithy apparently served as a social gathering-place here, because there were a good many nail kegs upended to serve as stools, and most of them were in use.

The locals who gave Longarm the eye as he rode nearer were all farmers, judging from their muddy shoes and mis-shapen hats.

Whatever conversation they'd been having ended abruptly when Longarm pulled to a halt in front of them.

And he would have to say that there wasn't a friendly expression turned in his direction.

Hell, he hadn't been here long enough to make any enemies that he knew about.

He responded to their suspicions with a smile and a touch of his hat brim. "Howdy, gentlemen. Mind if I step down?"

Someone grunted, and he decided that was close enough to being an invitation. He swung out of the saddle still smiling, but already he was hoping that not everybody in Beck City was as sour as these boys.

Chapter 13

Sure was a friendly crowd in Beck City, M.T. All but one
of the men looked at him like they thought he was fixing to
start asking them to loan him money. The lone exception
made a sour face and spat a stream of yellow tobacco juice
before he hitched up his jeans and consented to greet the
newcomer.

"Twenty cent a hoof for shoeing," he said. Yes, sir, a
hearty welcome indeed. And at that, the price he quoted was
double what it ought to be.

"Thank you for that information. I will keep it in mind
in case I need my horse shod. My name's Custis Long."
Longarm smiled pleasantly and extended a hand toward the
smith.

Not that Longarm would have guessed him for the Beck
City smith just from looking at him. He was short and of
slender build, although his arms and shoulders bulged with
wiry muscle. And he looked years too young to be a smith.
Not that there were any rules laid down on the subject, of

course; more like it was a matter of normal expectations of the kind that were not always realized.

The man blinked and hesitated for only a moment; then his innate courtesy took over from his suspicions and he took Longarm's hand. "Clete Miller," he said.

"Pleasure to meet you, Mr. Miller."

"Just Clete will do for me."

"Then you can call me . . . Custis." The slight falter in his voice was because he damn near said Longarm from pure habit. Except he wasn't supposed to be a lawman here and there really wasn't any other natural connection with the nickname other than the long arm of the law.

"You, uh, got business here, Custis?"

"Now that's something that I can't say yet, Clete. I'm looking around for grazing land. Won't know until I learn more about this country whether I'm here to do business or just to keep on riding and looking."

"Keep ridin'," a low voice muttered from somewhere off to the side.

"Pardon?"

Whoever it was who'd spoken didn't look up or otherwise admit to the fact. The farmers gathered outside Clete Miller's smithy were all studiously avoiding the visitor's eyes.

"Ah, don't pay them no attention, Custis. They're just a mite upset today," Miller offered.

"How's that, Clete?"

" 'Nuther damn robbery, that's how," a farmer with a black beard and no socks snapped. Miller nodded confirmation of the complaint.

"I see," Longarm said. "I'd have to admit that a stranger riding in right now could find himself under suspicion. And if the robbery occurred any time in the past minute or two, well, I'd say that I'd be a suspect, all right. I've sure been in town that long." He smiled.

"Wasn't in town," the farmer grumped. "Was out on the flats."

Wherever those were supposed to be. As close as Longarm could tell, just about everything he'd seen since he left the Missouri behind could justifiably be called the flats.

60

"Well, I'm sorry somebody got robbed," Longarm sympathized. "I hope nobody got hurt."

"Just a damn farmer. You cowmen don't much give a shit 'bout that, though, do you," the same man accused.

"Now, Birdy, you got no cause to fuss at the gentleman like that. He isn't the one done it," Miller said.

"Don't exactly know that, do we?" another farmer put in.

"Whoa, fellas," Longarm said patiently. He winked at Miller and smiled toward the unhappy farmers. "I can understand your suspicions, and I don't take any offense to them. But I'd rather they didn't get out of hand, if you see what I mean." He pulled out a pair of cheroots and offered one to the smith, then lighted the other and helped himself to a seat on one of the upended nail kegs.

"As for that remark about cowmen and farmers," he went on, "I imagine you've heard stories back East about feuds and whatnot. Is that so?"

He fixed the nearest man with a look and waited for the nod he knew pretty much had to come.

"Sure it's so," Longarm agreed then. "But I hope you don't believe quite everything you heard before you came out here to take up homestead ground in the basin. There've been feuds, true. But that sort of thing happens when farmers want to come in and claim homestead land on grass that cowmen have been using for years, some places for decades. Those cowmen might not have legal right to all they claim, but they come to think of it as their land anyhow. That's where the feuding and the fussing gets started. Here in the Judith, gentlemen, any cowmen you come across will be just as new to the country as you are. Nobody will have any expectation of more than he's entitled to, whether by claim or by purchase. So I don't think you have to worry about that sort of war here."

"You believe that, mister?"

"I do believe that. And the name's Custis. Mister Long was my dad."

The fellow smiled a little in spite of himself. He acted like he didn't much want to give up his hostility but was willing to accept it now that it was happening.

61

"Hell, I dunno. Maybe you're right."

"But we've sure had the idea that our problems've been with greedy cowmen."

"Gentlemen I don't think you'll find cowmen any greedier than anybody else. Including farmers."

"If it ain't cowmen, then who's doing it?"

"Doing what? Pulling off one robbery?" Longarm asked, already knowing the general answer but still short on the details.

That drew a round of snorts and grimaces from the men at Clete Miller's smithy.

"It's sure as hell more than just the one robbery, Custis," Miller said.

"I'd be interested in hearing about it," Longarm invited.

That was more than enough to open the floodgates. The men were bitter and wanted an excuse to talk anyway. Having an open-eared stranger handy to pour their troubles onto was all they needed.

"There's farms been burnt, Custis."

"Folks shot down in their own yards."

"Two ladies raped."

"Last week our bank was robbed. Cleaned plumb out."

"Joe Ackerton was murdered and now his widow's gone out of her mind. Why, we don't even know did anything happen to her that night 'cause she isn't in her right mind enough to tell us whatever she seen."

"It's gotten bad here, Custis."

"Was I you, mister, and didn't have seed in the ground an' all my hopes planted here already, I'd damn sure hitch the wagon and roll the hell outa here."

"If you're wise, Custis, you'll look elsewhere for your cows to graze."

"Far away from the damn Judith as you can get. That's my notion on the subject."

"Bloody country, this. They told us the Indian troubles was over an' the country safe. They lied when they said that, mister. The Injuns couldn't't've been half this amount of trouble."

That particular speaker, Longarm realized, had never seen

a war party coming at him or he wouldn't have been so sure of his statement.

"It really is bad, Custis," Miller agreed. "Worse than we looked for when we came in here."

"Isn't the law doing anything to protect you?" Longarm asked with feigned innocence.

That question, as much as the possible presence of Ambrose Warren in the Judith Basin, was exactly what had brought Longarm here.

He kept his voice and expression bland and neutral, though, and calmly drew on his cheroot while he waited for the farmers to gather up a fresh head of steam they might need to vent.

Chapter 14

"We ain't got no damn law," one man asserted.

"Bull," another snorted. "We got too damn much law."

"Now there's a difference of opinion for you," Longarm observed mildly. A few of the men smiled.

"What it comes down to," Clete Miller said, "is that we have law here. But I don't s'pose you could say it's been doing us much good."

Longarm raised an eyebrow and exhaled a stream of pale smoke.

"There's a town marshal—"

"Appointed by Mr. Beck," the man called Birdy injected.

"—who isn't so much a bad marshal as that he's young and inexperienced," Miller went on as if there had been no interruption. "Just a kid, actually. A nice kid, mind, but still just a kid. And as new to this country as we are."

Longarm nodded. It could make a difference. He'd known sixteen-year-olds he would trust to pick up a gun and stand back to back with him anytime, and men in their middle age who he wouldn't trust to not shoot their own ears off. But the ones who could be trusted were generally men, or boys, who had seen some country and knew trouble and could deal with both when they had to. The age didn't matter, but experience sure did.

"When we started having the troubles," Miller said, "we first asked the town marshal for help. But o' course he doesn't have anything to say about anything outside the town limits, and if there's a county organized yet, we don't know where or by who. It's one of the things we've all been too busy to think about much. So when we saw we needed help we wrote to this federal marshal fella up in Helena."

That would be Hall, of course, but Longarm wasn't supposed to know that yet.

"What did you ask him for?" Longarm asked.

"Help, o' course." A couple of the men looked at Longarm like they thought the question a rather stupid one, although he hadn't particularly thought so. Right often the answer to something is colored by the question that is asked. And a simple request for help isn't really the same thing as the blunt demand for an investigation into something specific.

"So what'd this federal fella do for you?"

"Damn little, that's what."

"He appointed us a U.S. deputy marshal, Custis," Miller said with a shrug.

"And that didn't help?"

"Shit, all he done, mister, was to send our town marshal a appointment as a fed'ral deputy too."

"Which means he's got what they call joorishdiction now," another man added.

"Which means now he rides out t' wherever something has happened an' he looks around an' says yeah, poor sonuvabitch is dead all right. Or whatever. But he don't actually do any more than he already done."

"Big help it was t' write to that federal fella in Helena."

"Government don't care about us nohow," a bitter voice said. "They so-called give land away, but once we've got ourselves rooted here, they try an' tax it back away from us. Let me tell you something, mister cowman, the worst damn thing ever happened to this country was that free-land-giveaway scam they call the Homestead Act. All that act does is prove the old saying, mister. There ain't no such thing as a free lunch. One way or another a fella ends up paying."

"Through the nose," another agreed.

"Up the ass is more like it."

"Sons o' bitches don't even grease the stick first."

Longarm rubbed his chin and sighed. Sitting here and listening to invective and bitterness wasn't going to accomplish very much. What he needed first was a room and a shave. Then he probably ought to meet this federal deputy and the town leaders.

Normally his first duty on entering an area where there was already a U.S. deputy would be to introduce himself formally and let the local man know there was another peace officer operating in his jurisdiction. This one was outside the norm, though. Marshal Hall wasn't supposed to know that he was under suspicion from the Justice Department.

Even so, Longarm wanted to meet the young man who was his counterpart in the Judith Basin.

"I didn't see a hotel when I rode in," he observed. "Any ideas where I might find a room?"

"You figure to stay, do you?"

Longarm shrugged. "Long enough to ride around and look at the grass and the prospects." He smiled. "Long enough to buy a good meal for sure."

"You can get the meal at Troy Tate's place. He runs the first general store on your right, and his wife has started serving meals in the side room. Troy built the thing thinking to rent it out to another storekeeper, but so far nobody's been interested. And no wonder. The whole town's gonna die if something isn't done to make things better around here. Anyhow, Mrs. Tate will feed you for a fair price. You might ask them about a room too."

"Thanks." It was too soon to form any firm opinions about conditions in the Judith Basin, Longarm realized, but conditions in this particular piece of it sure seemed

66

to be on the shaky side. Beck City was having a power of troubles.

"If you don't mind," he said as he stood, "I might want to drop back and talk to you boys some more. You have some interesting things to say about what I can expect here."

"You won't likely find so many of us here usually, mister. We gathered in like this today 'cause we're all so upset by the robbery. Come together to see could we think of something we could do about it."

"I hope it isn't a vigilance committee you're talking about here," Longarm cautioned. Committees of vigilance were a fine idea. For about fifteen minutes. Then no matter how justifiable and noble they seemed at the beginning, they degenerated into mobs. And it was generally some innocent who ended up dangling at the end of a lynch rope. Longarm had seen it too many times before to ever want to see it again.

"Huh?"

He smiled. Good. If these farmers fresh arrived from the settled East had never so much as heard about a committee of vigilance, so much the better. Now he was only sorry he'd ever opened his mouth to mention it. "Never mind," he said.

"Sure, whatever."

"Reason I came down here to begin with, Clete," he said, "is that I need a place to keep my horse while I'm in town. Do you handle that sort of thing?"

"I do. I can put 'im in the corral there. He'll have grass hay and water. Grain would be extra if you want it."

"The hay and water will be fine." The roan wasn't accustomed to grain anyway, and likely wouldn't be used so hard that any would be necessary.

"I'll take care of him for you, Custis."

"Thanks, Clete." Longarm left his saddle and bridle at the smithy and carried the rest of his things with him. He left the unhappy farmers with a smile and a touch of his hat brim, then ankled toward town and the Tate store.

Chapter 15

Mrs. Tate's cafe was the one he'd spotted on his way into town. It was tucked tight against the side of one of the stores, but he hadn't realized the two businesses were part of the same outfit. The store part of the building had a higher roofline. The cafe side must have been added after the fact. Both, though, were made of milled lumber. Mr. and Mrs. Tate apparently had come to Beck City with the intention of staying.

There was no one in the cafe when Longarm entered it, not surprising since it was about midway between the lunch and dinner hours. A connecting door went through to the store. Longarm poked his head in there and saw a middle-aged couple perched on stools on either side of the store counter. They were playing a card game of some sort. Despite the name, assuming these were the Tates, both looked like they might have Scandinavian ancestry. Both the man and the woman were tall and blond and handsome, graying hair barely discernible in the naturally pale yellow as they aged.

"Hello?"

The woman turned with a smile of greeting. The man grimaced, then smiled too. "I suppose you've come looking for something to eat," he said.

"Yes, sir."

"I should've known it. First good hand I've drawn all afternoon, and what happens?" His grin said he wasn't really very upset about the interruption.

"If I'd known I would've waited," Longarm offered.

"Well, I wish you had. You know how dang women are. Let one of them win at something, and they crow about it for a week. Now she'll be insufferable." The woman in question laughed and made a face at her husband. She twitched a hip toward him and came across the crowded store floor to greet the customer. The Tates had a good marriage, Longarm figured, if they were teasing even in front of strangers.

He grinned and introduced himself, remembering this time that it was Custis and not Longarm he'd best be known by.

"Our pleasure, Mr. Long. I'm Maud Tate. The poor loser over there is my husband Troy."

"Ma'am. Mr. Tate." Longarm tipped his hat and stepped out of the doorway so Maud Tate could enter the empty cafe.

"Is it a meal you need, Mr. Long, or just coffee?"

"A meal if it's not too much trouble. The lunch I had was early and poor."

"I don't serve a regular menu, just whatever I can put together."

"I'm sure that will be fine, ma'am."

"It will take me a few minutes. You can go buy something from Troy while you're waiting. It will make him feel better about losing to his betters." She winked and disappeared into the kitchen.

Longarm took her advice at least to the extent of wandering into the store while he waited. There was nothing he needed to buy, so he took over the stool Maud Tate had just vacated and chatted with her husband to pass the time.

69

He gave the storekeeper the story of being a cowman come to the Judith in search of graze.

"Mostly farmers here, of course, Mr. Long," Tate said, "though I don't see why this country wouldn't be just as good for cattle if a man could get title to enough of it. Expensive doing it that way, though. The attraction for most of the people here is that the land comes cheap. You try to buy it outright, it's pretty dear."

"True, but cheap land is getting harder and harder to find," Longarm agreed.

"Impossible to find back home in Minnesota," Tate said.

"That what brought you here?"

Tate grinned. "Naw. I'm no farmer. I doubt I could raise a decent crop of weeds. Maud and me picked up and moved our store out here just because we wanted to. The idea of a fresh, new country appealed to us, and we'd read about the land openings here. We just up and sold whatever we couldn't move and packed whatever we could."

"It doesn't sound like you have any regrets."

The storekeeper shrugged. "Ask me next year."

"I spoke with some men over at the smithy. They didn't sound so happy with things."

"Don't blame them. I'd be nervous in their shoes too, but so far things have been pretty calm here in the town. Except for the bank being robbed, that is."

"They mentioned something about that. You haven't had any trouble, though?"

"Not a bit of it, knock on wood." He rapped his knuckles on the side of his head and grinned. "I guess Maud and me have been lucky. And of course this robber gang is pretty dumb."

"Oh?"

"Sure. Think about it," Tate said. "Except for the bank and a few stagecoach holdups, they've mostly been hitting the farms for their robberies. Now you tell me, Mr. Long. Is a farmer going to have more cash money laying around in the sugar bowl or is it in a store where you'll find the cash receipts waiting to be stolen? That's why I say they're dumb." The grin flashed again. "Though I'm grateful to be able to say it, you understand."

"Yes, sir, I would think so. I—"

"Mister?" The voice from the cafe was shy. Longarm turned. An uncommonly pretty girl of eighteen or so was standing there.

"Marta, this is Mr. Long. Mr. Long, our daughter Marta."

"Miss." Longarm tipped his hat to the girl.

"Your lunch is ready, Mr. Long. Mama said I should tell you or Daddy would keep you here talking until it got cold."

"We can't let that happen." Longarm excused himself and followed Marta into the cafe.

He had to admit that the view when he was walking behind her was almighty fetching.

Marta Tate was as blond as her mother and even more buxom. Not in the same category as Miss Day, of course. But then Longarm had seen prominent landmarks out on the flat plains lands that couldn't compare with Miss Day's tits.

Marta had a nicely rounded rump and a tiny waist and a peaches-and-cream complexion. Her cheeks were round and dimpled and her eyes a bright, wide blue. Altogether a *very* pretty girl.

"Sit anywhere you like, Mr. Long. I'll bring it out to you."

"Yes, ma'am."

She paused and gave him a searching look, then smiled and hurried off toward the kitchen.

Longarm helped himself to a corner chair where he could keep an eye on both the street and the side doors, and made himself comfortable.

Marta was back a moment later carrying a plate heaped with slices of roast meat—although just what kind of meat Longarm wouldn't have ventured a guess just from looking at it—and vegetables. She had a cup of coffee in her other hand and some utensils in her apron pocket. She was biting at her lower lip, the pink tip of her tongue protruding just a little, as she concentrated on not spilling the overly full coffee cup.

Very carefully she set the coffee down first, then came around beside him to put the plate in front of him. With him seated in the corner it would have been much simpler for her to stand beside the table and reach across with everything. Instead she wedged herself in close before she put the plate down. Then she leaned low enough that her breasts were pressing against his upper arm while she put the tableware down.

Her free hand trailed lightly over the back of his neck when she stood upright again.

Longarm looked at her. It might just have been his imagination, but he thought he saw something more than he would have expected in those large, innocent eyes.

Marta blushed but didn't look away.

"We have a storeroom behind the kitchen, Mr. Long. We aren't using it for anything. Daddy might be willing to put a cot in there and rent the room out. If you were looking for a place, that is." Her cheeks colored a deeper shade of rose, but still she held his eyes and would not look away.

He smiled. "Maybe I'll ask him about that, Miss Tate."

"If you like," she said. She touched his shoulder briefly, then hurried away toward the kitchen.

Longarm watched her depart. Interesting. Mighty interesting, he conceded. Then he gave his attention to the meal Marta's mother had prepared for him.

72

Chapter 16

Longarm leaned back from the table and lighted an after-lunch cheroot. He was hoping it would be the attractive—and obviously interested—Marta who came out to clear the table, but it was her mother who appeared instead. "Mighty good groceries, ma'am, thank you."

Maud smiled prettily and began piling the dirty dishes onto a tray.

"Your daughter mentioned that you might have a room to let?"

The lady frowned. "I can't imagine where she . . . oh, the storage room?"

"I think that's what she said, ma'am."

"I hadn't thought about it, but yes. There's no reason why that couldn't work. And Lord knows we could use a little extra cash. Troy!"

The lady and her husband went into consultation, and a few minutes later Longarm had a place to stay while he was in Beck City.

"I'll have it set up ready for you in half an hour, Mr. Long," Tate assured him. "Less if you're in a hurry."

"No hurry. I want to nose around and get acquainted with the town some this afternoon."

"That will be just fine then," Tate said with a smile.

They worked out a reasonable rate for the room with meals included, and Longarm paid for a week in advance. Then he wandered out onto the street and let the Tates get busy with whatever preparations they had to make for their new boarder's quarters.

City Hall was his first stop. The two-story sod structure turned out to be more show than substance. Apparently whoever planned and built it had assumed there would be more need for local administration than was the case here. The downstairs held one desk and one filing cabinet and no employees. A sign pointed up the staircase toward the town marshal's office. No one was up there either.

Longarm didn't bother to call out. There were only the two rooms in the place, the city hall part downstairs and the marshal's part upstairs.

The marshal's floor held another desk, three unoccupied chairs, and an iron-barred cage in a back corner where prisoners presumably would be confined. The cage would be suitable for penning a captured bear maybe, but wasn't much shakes for holding humans. It was a cube that was roughly five feet by five by five. Not big enough to stand in and too small to lie down in except catty-corner. Longarm hoped the town had gotten a bargain when they bought the device because it was no bargain otherwise. He shook his head and started back down the stairs.

"What d'you think you're doing up there?" The voice came from a young man who was standing in the doorway. The fellow looked vaguely familiar, although if Longarm had ever seen him before, he sure couldn't recall a place or a name to go with him.

"Looking for the town marshal," Longarm told him, continuing down to the bottom of the stairs.

"That's me. Marshal of Beck City, also deputy United States marshal."

Longarm nodded and introduced himself, spinning the same yarn that he was a cowman from Colorado come north to look for more graze.

"We don't need cows around here and we need a bunch of rowdy cowboys even less," the local marshal said without bothering to return the courtesy of an introduction.

"Really?" Longarm said.

"Really."

"Now that's interesting. First community I ever came across that didn't want fresh meat and a steady payroll handy." Longarm shrugged and reached for a fresh cheroot.

"Proves that a fella can learn something every day, don't it," the marshal said.

"Yes, sir, I'm sure it does. But I'm still interested in this country. Would you mind answering a few questions for me?"

"I'm busy. Another time," the marshal said curtly.

Longarm's lips thinned just a little. He could well imagine when that "other time" might be. About the same time that Hell froze over and both parties could skate to the table. The man's attitude, though, rankled. Just for the pure perversity of it Longarm smiled happy and innocent and asked, "And when exactly would that be, Marshal?"

The marshal gave Longarm a suspicious look to see if he was being ragged, but all he could spot in Longarm's expression was innocence and a sincere and open interest. He scowled. "Tonight, mister. Maybe I can talk t' you tonight."

"Thank you, Marshal. I appreciate that." Longarm smiled and bobbed his head and touched the brim of his Stetson. "See you later, Marshal." He left City Hall with his spur-jinglers jingling and went back out onto the street.

Funny, he reflected as he finally got around to lighting the cheroot. Now why wouldn't a new town want folks to come in and provide them with spending money and an availability of fresh beef?

Scared of Eastern stories about cowmen and farmers having to feud with each other? Maybe. Except this marshal, whoever he was, didn't look much like a recently transplanted Easterner himself. He looked like he might ought to know better.

Longarm shrugged and decided not to worry about one man's opinions anyhow. People could get their backs up about the damnedest things. It was likely something as simple as the marshal remembering a cowboy beating him up once.

Longarm walked the few short steps to the bank building, but found he was too late to meet the town's leading citizen there. It was past the middle of the afternoon, and the bank door was already locked and the blind pulled down. Later would have to be good enough.

He settled instead for taking a brisk stroll up and down the few streets of Beck City.

Not that there was so very much to see. With two exceptions the houses were small and new and ordinary.

The exception was what passed in Beck City for the proverbial Mansion on the Hill, which damn near every place has to have.

In this case the effect was spoiled some by the fact that the only "hill" available from one horizon to the next was a knoll that didn't rise more than four feet above the rest of the flat terrain.

Perhaps because of that disappointment, the owner of the home made up in grandeur what he lacked in elevation. The house was similar to the bank; it had a brick first floor and a wood second story and chimneys on either end. A porch ran across the full front of the place, and there was a carriage house out back that was two stories also, the top probably being used to store hay.

In Denver or San Francisco the place wouldn't have been any great shakes, but here it looked pretty grand. It pretty much had to be the banker's home, Longarm figured.

Off on the fringes of town opposite from the banker's place, there was another house that Longarm decided served a very different function for the community. That one wasn't particularly grand, though. In fact in daylight it was kind of squalid. It was a low, rambling, sod affair that ran in ells

76

and wings in several direction at once. There were hitch rails out front to accommodate a good many horses, and a red lantern was hung prominently beside the doorway. At this time of day the whorehouse looked empty, and there was no smoke rising from the chimneys.

Likely the girls would be getting up soon and having their breakfast, ready to start the night's business dealings.

The place looked bigger than Longarm would have expected to find in a town so new and so small.

But then farmers were an earthy lot anyway. Maybe the proprietor of the whorehouse knew something Longarm didn't.

Longarm took his look through the town and around it, and wound up by heading back toward Clete Miller's smithy and the farmers who were gathered there.

He was almost to the place when a commotion broke out on the street as a small, hysterical boy mounted on a brown mule came larruping into Beck City at a dead run.

Chapter 17

"Murder! There's been a murder!" the boy was shouting. Longarm broke into a run as the youngster tried to stop his mule. The animal by now was as panicky as the boy and refused to respond to the plow bit in its mouth. It seemed bent on heading south to Wyoming no matter what its rider wanted.

Longarm tried to grab the reins. The mule shied violently to the side, toppling the boy from his precarious bareback seat and sending him thumping into the dust. Kids bounce, fortunately, and this one was too excited to pay attention to minor injuries in any event. He was back on his feet and running toward City Hall almost without pause. One of the farmers who was running behind Longarm succeeded in claiming the loose reins and bringing the mule to a halt, but by then everyone else on the street, Longarm included, was intent on racing after the hysterical child.

The boy, Longarm, and half the rest of the population of Beck City thundered into City Hall. The town marshal met them all at the bottom of the stairs.

"There's been a murder, Mr. Barnes, sir," the boy blurted out. "Out on the road, sir. The stagecoach, sir. A passenger's been murdered." He managed to get it all out without taking a fresh breath, which made what he was saying progressively more difficult to understand. Still, it was clear enough. Too damn clear, really.

"What's this now, boy?" the marshal demanded.

"Murder, sir. Out on the road. The stage has been held up an' a passenger killed. Pap and me were in the field. We heard the shots. Seen two riders stop the stage an' heard the shooting. We run over there but we was too late t' help, Mr. Barnes, sir. That passenger's dead an' both leaders in the team was shot down. Pap throwed me onto Achilles an' told me t' come tell you quick."

A murmur of anger ran through the crowd that had gathered inside City Hall.

"Get after 'em, Jeff," someone said. "This happened recent, Tommy?"

"Yes, sir, Mr. Birdwell. No longer 'n it took me 'an Achilles to get here from our farm."

"Crane's farm isn't five mile out," the farmer named Birdwell, known as Birdy, said quickly. "They can't have gotten far. Which way'd they ride, Tommy?"

"South, sir. They took off t' the south."

"Get your horses, boys," the marshal ordered. "We'll start a posse and cut southwest. Maybe we can head them if we're quick. Don't take time to grab anything but your guns; we'll be riding hard and fast."

Marshal Barnes—had to be kin to Danny and Lute Barnes, Longarm figured, which was why the marshal had seemed so familiar when Longarm first saw him—was already hurrying into motion himself, running back up the stairs for a rifle or something while the other men dashed out toward Clete Miller's place and whatever mounts they could grab.

Longarm, however, hung back with young Tommy Crane, who was being ignored in this new surge of excitement. Longarm put a hand on Tommy's shoulder and pulled him out of the way when Marshal Barnes came charging down the stairs at a dead run and leaped off the third or fourth step in his rush to get out to his horse.

"You can calm down now, son," Longarm said gently. "You did just right."

The boy gave him a worried look. "Did I?"

"Nobody could've done better," Longarm assured him.

"Pap tol' me to haul my ass, sir. I, uh, never heard him talk like that before now."

"It's a serious thing that happened, Tommy. Your pap was excited and wanted to get the right thing done right away. You both did fine about this."

The kid nodded. Longarm pulled out a cheroot and guided Tommy with him as he walked over to the doorway. Down the street the posse was already being assembled, most of the men holding rifles and shotguns, very few of them with handguns. The excitement of the humans was transmitted quickly to the horses so that there was considerable crow-hopping and kicking going on.

"You ain't going with them, sir?"

Longarm smiled. "I don't think they need me right now. Maybe I could be useful helping your pap, though. Would you show me where this happened?"

"Yes, sir."

"Good."

Longarm knew that the posse had damned little chance of capturing the coach robbers and that what little chance they had would neither be hurt nor helped by the presence of one more gun in the crowd.

Little chance, he figured, because Marshal Jeff Barnes was pinning his hopes on speed to catch the felons when it was staying power that was needed.

Sheer, stubborn determination—along with a good tracker—was what was required to chase down a murderer on the run.

Speed depended on plain old luck to intercept a trail. It could happen, of course, but only a fool counted on it. Better to plan for a long, slow chase than to hope for a quick one.

In Longarm's opinion the town would have been better

served if the marshal and his posse had taken all the time they needed to gather bedrolls and supplies and their most durable horses, and then sworn they wouldn't be back until the murderers were in custody. If that took a week, two weeks, what matter? The way Barnes was going about it they would either have the murderers within an hour or not at all.

And the likelihood was that it would be not at all.

Longarm didn't figure he needed to observe that while it was happening. And he might be able to accomplish something out at that crippled stagecoach.

"Come along, son."

The mule Tommy had ridden into town was tied at a hitch rail halfway down the next block. Longarm collected it and walked on down to Miller's smithy to reclaim his horse and saddle.

The posse by then was half a mile out of town and raising a cloud of dust as they went hell-bent for leather off toward the southwest.

In this flat country they would be visible for several miles, but Longarm was not paying any attention to them now. He genuinely wished them all well, and conceded that young Barnes was doing the best he knew how to catch the murderers. But Longarm wasn't counting on any of that.

"All right, Tommy," Longarm said once he was mounted. "Show me the way."

Chapter 18

Longarm sent young Tommy and his mule Achilles home as soon as he had the stagecoach in view. The boy acted relieved that he wouldn't have to see the blood close up.

"Howdy," Longarm said to the men on the ground as he rode up to the scene.

It was bloody enough, all right. Just like the boy had said, both leaders in the coach team had been shot down in their traces. The road near them was slippery with fresh blood.

Dead livestock, though, came under the category of nuisance, not tragedy. The tragedy lay nearby in another pool of dust-filmed fresh blood. A man's body lay stretched out there with a lap robe covering him. All Longarm could see of the dead man was his shoes, which were expensive and highly polished footwear suitable for city streets instead of farms or rough country. The dead man hadn't been any laborer or farmer or cowboy.

"Who are you?" the coach driver asked suspiciously.

"Name's Long," Longarm told him. "Figured I might be some help out here while the posse is chasing whoever did this."

"Not much t' be done, I expect," said a man in overalls who Longarm assumed would be Tommy's father Crane. "We 'bout got it under control now."

"So I see. Mind if I step down?"

"Go ahead," the driver said.

The men already had the harness unfastened. It would have been quicker to cut the leather away, but the driver apparently was trying to salvage his company's equipment off the dead horses. The wheelers in the stage team were still nervous about being close to the smell of so much blood. While Crane and the driver went about rigging a drag on the first of the dead animals, Longarm backed the wheelers a few feet and swung them off the road so they could calm down.

A small mule that was a fair match for Achilles was hooked to a dead horse twice its size. It grunted and strained, and slowly the carcass began to slide on the grit and dust of the roadway.

"Just so's it's outa the road, Harry," the driver said.

"Right."

The two men seemed to have things under control, so Longarm took a moment to look inside the coach. There were no other passengers. Apparently the dead man had been the only passenger along for this run.

Two expensively fashioned leather suitcases were in the luggage boot. On the floor of the driving box there was a small carpetbag, probably the overnight kit carried by the driver, and an ironbound cash box. Longarm raised an eyebrow when he saw that.

Crane and the driver managed to skid the first horse clear of the public road, then unhooked the little mule and came back to haul the second carcass out of the way.

Longarm hunkered down beside the human body and pulled the lap robe back.

The dead man was a handsome, nicely dressed man in his late thirties or early forties. He wore a tailored charcoal gray suit with matching vest, and had a diamond stickpin in the knot of his tie. The watch chain suspended across the front of his vest was gold and was attached to a railroad-grade timepiece in a solid gold hunt case. An inscription inside the cover of the watch read: "To K.M. from C."

"You want t' see if he has any gold teeth you c'n knock out an' put in your pocket too, neighbor?"

Longarm looked up to see the coach driver giving him the eye. Either the driver was an honest man who wanted to preserve his dead passenger's personal effects for return to the family . . . or the man wanted to lift them himself. Longarm gave him a tight smile in return and tucked the watch back where he had gotten it.

He had to be careful to avoid soiling his fingers with the dead man's blood. The front of his chest was dark and matted with the stuff.

Longarm undid the tie, vest, and shirt and pushed the cloth aside. There were two wounds punched into the flesh just above heart level. Either would have killed him instantly. A playing card would have covered both of them.

"You want to tell me what happened here, please?" Longarm asked.

The driver came over closer and squatted. "Why should I tell you, mister?"

"You don't have to. I'm just trying to think constructively here."

"I . . . aw, hell, man, I'm sorry. Kinda touchy today. You know?"

"Sure." Longarm began searching the dead man's coat pockets, looking for some form of identification on the body.

"I mean, I never lost a passenger before. Can't say as I like it, neither."

"Don't blame you," Longarm agreed. He found a slim wallet and pulled it out, but gave the driver his attention for the time being.

"What happened . . . and it don't make no sense . . . is that we was driving along like usual, and this here pair of riders was coming towards us. In plain sight, they was.

84

Hell, I'd seen 'em coming for three miles or more. They were coming at a walk, not hurrying and not doing nothing that looked funny. Two guys wearing big hats and dusters, like they was dressed for long-haul travel. I mean, I pass two dozen like that every day of my life. You know?"

Longarm nodded. He understood what the driver was really saying. The man was trying to tell himself that he couldn't have foreseen this and that it wasn't his fault that his passenger was dead now.

"They get up to me an' when they look up I see that they're wearing masks under those hats. A pink, tan kinda color the masks were, which is prob'ly why I didn't notice them before. You know?"

Longarm nodded. Crane had come close and was listening too now, although probably he had heard the story at least once already. Before midnight everyone in Beck City would have heard it. The only question was whether this coach driver would ever start to believe that he wasn't at fault for his passenger's murder.

"Before I knew what was up, they pulled their dusters open an' showed carbines, real short-barreled ones, that they'd been carrying slung alongside their legs under those dusters."

"Well, I seen what was up *then*, all right. I brung the coach to a stop. That's company policy. If you can't run an' can't fight, then don't do nothing that would cause a passenger to get hurt. Don't offer resistance when you got no chance of it helping matters."

Longarm nodded. It was a sensible policy.

"So I bring the coach to a stop, an' the one on the left motions with the barrel of his gun that I should climb down. So I do. The guy motions again toward the coach, so I open the door an' this fella here gets down. My passenger, damned if he didn't look excited. Like the idea of being robbed was . . . I hate t' say this, but he acted almost like he was *enjoying* it." The driver shook his head sadly.

"It could be," Longarm said. "He looks like he's an Eastern fella. He might've read about highwaymen and Western badmen and thought it romantic or something."

85

"Yeah, maybe that was the way he saw it. I mean, the whole way down here he was moving from one side of the coach t' the other, looking out the windows at every little thing. I could feel the rig shift every time he done that, of course. Earlier this afternoon we passed a couple mangy buffalo an' the guy like to wet himself. He shouted right out loud. So maybe that was it."

"You were saying . . . ?"

"The murder. Right. Them two had us both get down on the ground. The one of them came up close an' stood right over us. The other went over to my team. Naturally I figure they're gonna lift the money box, which has the mail pouch in it too, but instead of that the one by the team ups with that carbine and shoots. First my near leader, then the off. Shot them in the head an' dropped them right down.

"The wheelers begin squealing and carrying on, and naturally I'm looking at them and thinking I should run try and gentle them but wondering if I'd be shot if I done that.

"Then I hear a shot, right beside me practically, and my passenger is down on the ground. The son of a bitch killer turns his horse half around so he can take careful aim and shoots into this fella's chest again.

"Well, naturally I figure I'm next. But neither of them two did a thing more. Never said a word to me, never so much as pointed a carbine in my direction. They nodded to one another, turned their horses, and started fogging it off in that direction there." He turned and pointed in a south-by-southeast direction.

"Harry and his boy, they were in that field right over there. They seen what happened and came running. I expect you know the rest."

Longarm frowned. "They never tried to grab the cash box?"

"No, sir. Far as I could see they never so much as looked at it."

"They never said what they wanted?"

"Mister, they never said *nothing*. Neither one of 'em opened his mouth that I could hear. They waved those gun barrels to get me and this man down off the coach. They

86

neither one of them ever spoke so much as a word. Shot down my leaders and this gentleman and rode right away. For no *reason*. That's the crazy thing. They had no reason for this but meanness, mister. None."

Longarm grunted and glanced down at the wallet he was holding.

It held cash—a good bit of it in large bills, although Longarm didn't bother to count the money—and a thin sheaf of engraved business cards belonging to a Karl Meek, field representative for the Lakeside National Protective Association. Whatever a field representative was, and whatever the Lakeside National Protective Association was supposed to be. The company address given was in Chicago.

Longarm thumbed one of the business cards out and handed it to the coach driver. "I expect someone has to write a letter to these people telling them what happened to their man Meek," he suggested.

The driver shuddered but took the card. "That ain't a job I want, mister."

"No, but it wasn't your fault," Longarm told him truthfully. "Mr. Meek was shot down deliberate. It had nothing to do with you."

"But . . . "

"Listen to me now. Are you listening?"

The unhappy driver nodded.

"If it was pure meanness involved here, if it was just that two fellas came out today and decided it would be fun to kill somebody, they would've shot your wheelers and you too. But they didn't do that, did they?"

"No, they didn't, thank God."

"Right. They didn't. What they did was to lay for this coach and shoot down Mr. Meek here on purpose. I can't tell you why, but it was cold-blooded and deliberate. An execution, you might say. You had nothing to do with that, mister. Your leaders they shot just to keep you stopped here so they could get away. Maybe they didn't count on Mr. Crane and his boy being close. Why, maybe the posse out of Beck City will have caught them by now." Longarm smiled, wanting to give the coach driver something positive to think about even though there was slim chance that the two murderers would have been bagged.

"I sure as hell hope so."

"So do we all." Longarm took the wallet and Meek's watch and chain and handed them to the driver, this time giving him a responsible task to carry out. "I suggest you put these in the cash box for safekeeping. You can send all his things along with that letter to Chicago, right?"

"Yeah, that's . . . that's a good idea."

"Come on. I'll help you put Mr. Meek's body into the coach and follow you into town. The wheelers should be able to pull that easy enough by themselves."

"They won't like it, but they'll manage it okay," the driver said. He seemed to feel better now that things were getting back onto a course he could understand and cope with. "Harry, you and this gentleman put Mr. Meek inside the coach while I take the loose harness off and get my rig ready t' roll again. Careful of him now." The driver was definitely doing better now that he was able to take charge of something again.

Longarm and Tommy's father quickly moved to comply with the driver's orders. Longarm took a moment extra to pick up the empty brass cartridges that had been ejected from the carbines. There were only two, implying that the murderers hadn't bothered to chamber fresh rounds again once their killing was done. Both were ordinary .44-40 brass, available anywhere and as common as dirt. The stagecoach was able to roll behind its abbreviated team again within five minutes.

Chapter 19

The slow-moving stagecoach was met in town by a slender, bespectacled young man wearing a business suit and a worried expression.

"I heard you had trouble, Cal. Is it true? Someone was murdered?"

"'Fraid so, Mr. Beck," the driver said. "Fella from Chicago. Two sons o' bitches with carbines gunned him down right in front of my eyes."

"Damn," Beck complained. "I wish . . . " He didn't bother to finish the sentence. His frustration and anguish were obvious.

Longarm hung back, not wanting to intrude as Beck and the coach driver discussed what they ought to do with Meek's body. There was a storekeeper in town who doubled as barber and undertaker, but he was out riding with the posse at the moment. Between them the banker and coach driver concluded that they should take the body to the undertaker's back room and lay him out there. Meek could be tended to later.

Beck, Longarm saw, was an unlikely leading citizen.

The banker couldn't yet have seen the age of thirty, and he did not look at all the part of a community founder.

His hair was dark and slicked flat against a smallish head. He was clean-shaven, the overall effect of that being to hint that he really didn't need to shave yet. Say, once or twice a week at the most.

Longarm doubted the young man weighed a hundred twenty pounds, although he was at least of average height, and his wrists and neck were so thin they looked like they might snap in two just from the strains of everyday living. Pencil-pushing had to be what he was best at, so perhaps it was no wonder he'd become a banker. Maybe the rest of it, naming this new town after him, followed naturally on the heels of his being in that particular line of work.

Longarm and the driver carried Meek's body inside a small, cluttered store that had a tiny area set aside for an exceptionally tall-legged chair—a homemade barber chair, Longarm decided—and on through to a storage room where an old door had been laid on sawhorses. Apparently that was as close as Beck City could come to having a mortuary.

They laid Meek out with his hands folded and eyes held closed with large penny coins, and left him there to await the part-time undertaker.

The banker fluttered around in the background, directing and instructing and in general overseeing the procedure while Longarm and the driver did the actual work of carrying the dead man.

"Thanks, mister," the driver named Cal said when Meek and his luggage were safely in storage.

"Yes, indeed, sir. Our thanks to you." The young banker stepped forward with a smile and a handshake to finally greet Longarm.

"No problem, Mr. Beck. My name is Long, sir. Cu—"

The banker's eyes went wide, and his smile turned into a huge grin. "Long, you say? Custis Long?"

"Why, yes, I . . ."

"By God, sir, I do owe you a debt of gratitude, don't I."

"You do?"

"But of course, Mr. Long. Egads, man, Loretta told me how helpful you were to her. Especially when . . . on the riverboat that night, you understand. You will forgive me, sir, if I don't want to mention particulars." Beck was still grinning, and now he was pumping Longarm's hand like he expected to draw water from one hell of a long ways down.

"You know Miss Day, I take it?" Longarm asked, pleased to be so welcome but still confused about just why he was.

"Know her? But of course I know her. Loretta is my fiancée after all, sir."

"But I thought . . . "

Beck threw his head back and laughed, all the while continuing to pump Longarm's arm. "But I'm Andrew, Mr. Long. Andy Beck."

"I thought Miss Day's fiancé was a Mr. Moresbeck."

The banker laughed again and explained. "I've shortened it since I left Kentucky, Mr. Long. A matter of simplification, you see. An old family habit, you might almost say. My people came to this country four generations ago from Slovakia, and we've been busy ever since that time trying to make our name easier to cope with. Why, even I can't get my tongue around what it used to be."

"I see," Longarm said. Although he didn't really.

Still, a man was entitled to be whoever and whatever he damn well said he was, just so long as his notions didn't run afoul of anybody else's rights and freedoms.

If Andrew Moresbeck wanted to call himself Andy Beck—or Abraham Lincoln, for that matter—it was all right with Custis Long.

"Pleasure to meet you, Andy," Longarm muttered.

"Dinner," Beck cried. "Are you free for dinner . . . no, wait. Not tonight. I almost forgot a prior arrangement. Tomorrow night then. Surely you can join Loretta and me for dinner tomorrow. Please say you will, Mr. Long."

"Well, yeah, I reckon I could do that, Mr. Beck."

"Andy," the banker insisted.

"If you'll call me Custis, Andy."

"Custis it is, sir." Andy Beck gave Longarm's hand a few final pumps and relinquished it. Just in time too. Longarm's whole arm was beginning to ache. The young banker didn't have much of a grip but he was hell for persistent. "Tomorrow evening, Custis. At six? Loretta will be so excited. She's spent much of our afternoon telling me about you. Why, I daresay I was beginning to think I should become jealous, Custis."

Longarm smiled. "Funny, Andy. The whole way up the river from Omaha, Miss Day talked only about you an' how much she was looking forward to being with you."

Andy chuckled and clapped Longarm on the shoulder. It was a gesture that Longarm didn't much favor when it came from strangers, but of course he didn't let that show to the exuberant and exhilarated young man.

"We can count on you to join us, then?"

Longarm nodded.

"Wonderful. Loretta will be thrilled."

Beck acted like he wanted to say more, but the conversation was interrupted by the arrival of a good many horses in the street outside. Cal had gone ahead from the mortuary into the store, and stepped back now to let Beck and Longarm know the posse was back.

"Did they . . . ?" Beck began.

"Don't know yet," Cal told him.

"Excuse us please, Custis." Beck and Cal hurried outside, and Longarm was right behind them.

Chapter 20

It didn't take much conversation to learn that the posse had come up a failure. The men rode back into town with their eyes down and their expressions glum. All the hustle and excitement of their leaving had been replaced now with drag-ass sluggishness and silence.

Longarm was far from being surprised. But this would have been a nice time to be proven wrong about something.

Marshal Barnes had been headed toward City Hall, but reined aside when he saw Andy Beck come out of the store. He stopped his horse in front of the banker, one very young man confronting another, and sadly reported in.

"Not a trace of them, Mr. Beck. Not one damn hoofprint."

Longarm pulled out a cheroot and lighted it, giving Barnes's report to Beck only half an ear while he looked off into the distance where the cold-blooded murderers were supposed to have been riding.

He thought briefly about stepping back into his saddle and riding out there himself to see if he could cut some sign.

He rejected the idea as quickly as it occurred to him.

It was nearly dusk already. By the time he could get a mile out of town it would be too dark to look for tracks.

Besides, contrary to popular mis-opinion, it was damn near impossible to track lightly burdened horses over dry grassland anyway. Especially in country like this where horses, wagons, mules, and domestic livestock were moving in and out of town and from farm to farm.

Even starting from the scene of the shooting and moving slowly and with exhaustive care, it probably would be impossible to trail the killers more than a mile or two.

Longarm figured he might try that longshot come daylight tomorrow, but for the time being there was nothing he could expect to accomplish.

Marshal Barnes and Andy Beck took the coach driver, Cal, with them back to City Hall so Barnes could get a full report on the murder, and Longarm headed to the nearer of the town's two saloons, along with most of the other men who had been out with the posse.

In the absence of any rye whiskey worth drinking he bought himself a beer, and propped a boot onto the bar rail and contented himself with listening while the possemen rehashed the useless chase.

Not that there was all that much to hear. Barnes apparently led them in a straight run south by east, and kept them moving hard and fast until the horses started to play out. Then the bunch turned around and came back at a slow pace.

Helluva plan the deputy United States marshal for the Judith Basin had come up with, Longarm thought with a highly critical professional eye to how things might have been done.

Run out and walk back. You bet. And raising a dust cloud every outbound step of the way.

If the killers had been dumb enough to keep going in that one same direction after they beat it from the stagecoach, they never would have been dumb enough to let themselves get caught by a posse acting that way. The posse's dust probably could've been seen for five miles or better.

Still, Longarm conceded, Jeff Barnes had likely done the best he knew how. The pity was that he just didn't know how.

Longarm supposed that was the sort of thing he needed to include in his report to the Attorney General. Marshal Hall had acted when he appointed Barnes as his deputy here, maybe even acted in good faith, and now Deputy Barnes seemed to be acting in good faith too.

One thing for sure. When it came to politics and the political hacks who were raised to high station by the system of payoff appointments, *nobody* ever got himself fired just for stupidity.

If this was the worst Longarm's report came up with, Marshal Hall and Deputy Barnes were safe in office for the rest of their days. Or until there was a change in Administration, whichever came first.

And as for the execution-style murder of Mr. Karl Meek, well, regrettable though that business was, it was not a federal crime and not a part of Longarm's jurisdiction. The mail pouch on Cal's coach hadn't been touched, and that was as deep as Longarm's interest was officially allowed to run.

Neither of the killers remotely fit with Ambrose Warren, after all, and Longarm's only interests here were supposed to be Brose Warren and Marshal Hall. Putting cuffs on the one and passing judgment on the other.

He figured that should be enough for him to chew on without shouldering all the rest of the burdens of this whole end of the Judith too.

He checked his watch and decided it was probably close to supper time. He'd best get back over to the cafe and claim his dinner before the posse crowd decided to clean the kitchen out.

Besides, there wasn't going to be much to learn here. And Marta Tate was over there at her folks' place.

Longarm couldn't help but be more than a little bit interested in that.

He stepped outside and ambled down the street toward the Tate store and cafe and impromptu boardinghouse as dark fell over Beck City, Montana.

Chapter 21

Again, because so many of the townspeople were still in the saloon rehashing the day's events, Longarm had the cafe nearly to himself.

Maud Tate brought the plates of food out to him, but from across the room young and pretty Marta made it clear with eye and body language that the lean and handsome visitor was not unnoticed. Or unappreciated.

A definite stroke of good fortune this, getting a spare room in the Tate establishment, he decided.

Longarm lingered over supper and coffee afterward, enjoying a smoke and the scenery alike as now the place began to fill with men who were leaving the saloon and wanted to eat before they started home.

"Mind if I join you, Mr. Long?"

Longarm looked up. Troy Tate was standing beside the table, hopefully oblivious to the inspection Longarm had just been giving to his daughter's ass.

"Please." Longarm pushed a chair away from the table for him.

"One of the few bad things about Maud opening the cafe," Tate said, "is that we never get to sit down and take our meals with the family all together. Used to be . . . " His face twisted just a little as he hesitated; some old but not forgotten pain, Longarm guessed. "Never mind." Tate brightened. "Are you finding the prospects here attractive?" he asked.

"Too soon to say," Longarm told him. The response was honest as far as it went. Which wasn't particularly far, of course.

"Well, I for one hope you decide to locate here. We need all the growth we can get. If that is selfish of me, so be it. I want all the potential customers possible, and I'm sure the other merchants feel the same. I, uh, hope that incident this afternoon didn't put you off."

"Murder does tend t' be a little off-putting, don't it," Longarm said with a thin smile.

"True, of course. Although I overheard someone say that this was a deliberate thing and not the playful rowdiness we've been experiencing."

"Rowdiness?" Meek's was not the first murder to take place in this end of the Judith. And Custis Long for one tended to look at murder as being something a tad more serious than mere rowdiness.

"Oh, I realize there've been a few other incidents of a serious nature. But really, Mr. Long, most of these farmers are allowing themselves to be upset over nothing. They're very easily upset. Most of the incidents have been no more than boyish pranks."

"Do tell." Tate, he realized, would be wanting to minimize the dangers in the Judith, hoping to attract a cow outfit with its people and its payroll. The businessman wanted business. But even so . . .

"Pranks. Boys, and some girls too, which certainly gives you some idea of how little seriousness is truly involved, playing at being highwaymen. Laughing and joking with coach passengers and giving back nearly as

98

much as they take from anyone."

"Robbery is robbery, though, wouldn't you agree?"

"Of course. No one in the territory is more concerned with law enforcement and public safety than I, Mr. Long. It is just that I think a good many of our, um, agrarian friends become unnecessarily excited." Tate smiled reassuringly, and accepted the plate of supper Marta hurried over to put in front of him.

The girl stood beside her father and looked over the top of his head, meeting Longarm's eyes boldly. Troy Tate didn't notice.

Longarm watched the girl leave, then scrubbed the coal of his cheroot off onto his plate so Tate could eat his dinner without cigar smoke in his face.

The Beck City merchant, Longarm reflected, seemed fairly contemptuous of the farmers who were the basis of the economy here.

What Longarm could read in Tate's words, and more, in the man's tone of voice, hinted that perhaps the Tates felt themselves superior to men who grubbed in the dirt for their livelihood.

Odd indeed in a community like this one. So why had someone like Troy Tate chosen to come here? He had said earlier that they'd sold off their belongings back east . . . Wisconsin, was it? no, Minnesota, he'd said . . . and moved west on a whim. Apparently the move wasn't turning out to be as agreeable as they had hoped.

You had to give them credit, though. They were an ambitious family, willing to turn their hand to any business that could show a profit. First the store, then the cafe, and now taking in boarders as well.

Longarm blinked and absentmindedly reached for his now-cold cigar.

Just how ambitious *were* these Tates?

Troy Tate minimized the threat of crime in the Judith. And hadn't chosen to ride with the posse this afternoon. Troy Tate had a daughter just about of an age that she could herself be one of the happy-go-lucky band of stagecoach robbers.

It was just entirely possible that daughter Marta might be helping Daddy out by fetching home income from thievery.

Or was that reaching too far too soon?

Possibly. But it was something Longarm intended to tuck away in the back of his mind for future examination as he collected more information to try the half-born theory against.

Tate finished his supper quickly and pushed his plate away. Longarm offered him a cheroot, which Tate accepted, and relighted his own smoke too.

"You went out to the scene of that, uh, incident today, didn't you, Mr. Long?"

"Mm, hmm." Longarm smiled at Marta as the girl brought the coffeepot to give her father and their guest a refill.

"They say the deceased was a gentleman from Chicago?"

"That's right. Fella named Meek. Worked for some outfit called the Lakeside National Protective Association there."

"Lakeside?"

"You sound like you've heard of it."

"Of course I have. Why, I daresay most of our merchants here are familiar with the organization. Moreover, I suspect nearly everyone engaged in trade here is doing business with Lakeside."

"What are they, suppliers of some sort?"

"An insurance firm, Mr. Long," Tate said into a wreath of blue-white smoke that enveloped his head. "They underwrite our insurance coverage." He frowned. "I hope this Meek fellow wasn't coming here to cancel our policies. Surely not, though. We businessmen haven't had much in the way of claims. The stagecoach company might have been covered by Lakeside, though. And I'm quite certain the bank uses Lakeside. I do hope they aren't intending to raise our premiums."

Longarm wondered if "field representative" might be a polite way to say "insurance investigator."

If Karl Meek was coming here to hunt down Ambrose Warren's gang, that would be plenty enough reason for the man to be met and murdered.

100

If Warren and company had some way to know in advance that an insurance investigator was expected.

That seemed a mighty big if.

But it certainly wasn't beyond possibility.

Another detail to tuck away and remember, Longarm decided.

If nothing else, he figured, he could ask the Chicago offices of this Lakeside outfit who Meek had been and what his purpose here was to be.

Ask them, sure, but not quickly and not easily. There were no telegraph wires into the Judith yet. The nearest communications should be all the way up to Fort Benton, he suspected, or over at Great Falls, whichever of those was the closer.

"While I think about it, Mr. Tate, where's the post office here?" he asked.

"Andy Beck has it over in the bank building," Tate said. "He built in a separate little side room just for that, keeps it separate from his bank because of the difference in business hours, and got his teller appointed postmaster. If you want anything in the post office during banking hours, you just stick your head in the door at the bank side and John will come help you. Bank closes at two and the post office not until five, so you can find John in the post office side then."

"Thanks."

"Do you play backgammon, Mr. Long?"

"No. Sorry."

Tate looked disappointed. "I was hoping for some new blood in the game tonight. That Maud of mine is a fine woman, but I tell you she's vicious when you bring out a deck of cards or a gaming board."

"I heard that," she called from halfway across the cafe.

Tate grinned at her, then turned to give Longarm a wink.

"You'll pay for your incautious tongue, Mr. Tate," Mrs. Tate warned.

"Uh, oh," Tate said in a low voice. "I think I've gone and stepped in it now."

Longarm laughed. If the Family Tate were involved in

101

this crime spree with Ambrose Warren, they certainly managed to be pleasant about it.

They were really a very likable bunch.

And young Marta perhaps most of all?

"Reckon I'll go have a drink while the cafe crowd thins down," Longarm said, "then come back and enjoy the use of that bed you made up for me. Care to join me, Mr. Tate?"

"Thanks, but I'll want to keep the store open just in case. I never close until the last of Maud's customers are gone. Everybody knows if I'm not behind the counter they can find me here if they need anything. Don't want to miss any sales, you know."

"Another time perhaps." Longarm excused himself and went back out into the night.

Chapter 22

The sound of the soft, surreptitious footsteps was not unexpected.

Not unwelcome either.

Longarm lay in the narrow bed in the storeroom-become-bedroom and smiled.

It wasn't much past ten, but the rest of the establishment was dark and silent. The Tate family had their living quarters behind the store part of the building. Half an hour ago Longarm had heard Troy and Maud Tate put their backgammon board away and tell Marta good night.

By now the elder Tates were probably asleep.

Marta, he suspected, was not.

A glow of pale yellow candlelight appeared under the door to Longarm's room as the softly padding footsteps came closer.

Long habit made him rest one hand near the butt of the big Colt that was slung at the head of the bed. But he didn't honestly expect to need it.

Tonight, he figured, it would be another sort of gun that he would be using.

The doorknob twisted, and a dry hinge creaked as the door was pushed open.

Pretty Marta, wearing a floor-length cotton nightdress and carrying a pencil-thin taper, stood there.

She raised a finger to her lips. But hell, Longarm had no intention of shouting an alarm at this intrusion.

He smiled and pulled the sheet off him.

The girl was old enough and more than willing enough, and he wasn't fool enough to turn down a good thing so freely offered.

Damn, but she was a mouthful too.

She had unpinned her hair since supper and brushed it to a glossy, golden sheen. It cascaded down to lie across her breasts in a most fetching manner.

The modest nightdress was floor long and throat high and covered her to her wrists. But all that cloth was unable to hide the charms beneath.

Her breasts jutted high and firm and proud. The material was thin enough that he could see the sharp points of her erect nipples showing through. Longarm's erection bumped and throbbed. He shifted over to the far side of the bed to make room for company.

Marta gave him a coy, kittenish smile and came inside the small room.

She pushed the door closed slowly, careful to not raise a racket with the hinges, and set her candle down on top of the upended box that was serving as a bedside table.

Obviously she didn't mind having a light in the room, and Longarm was glad. This girl was too good-looking to ever be in the dark.

Marta seemed to be enjoying herself. She examined him as if savoring his reactions, then stepped back a pace so the light fell on her.

She posed in front of him, deliberate and provocative about it.

She turned, tossed her head, turned again, showing herself to him from all angles.

"Mmm," he murmured.

"Shh," she warned. "You'll wake them."

He nodded. Far as he was concerned, the girl could enjoy herself however she wished. If what she wanted was absolute silence, why not. He grinned at her.

Marta gave him a seductive lowering of her eyes, doing something else with her mouth that Longarm thought was supposed to look sexy. Actually it looked kinda silly in his opinion. Not that he was complaining.

She bent and picked up the hem of her nightdress. With a canary-eating smile she straightened a little. Then a little more. As she came slowly upright one small stage at a time, she exposed more and more of what she had to offer.

Her feet were small and her ankles slender. Her calves were shapely and her knees dimpled. Her thighs were slender and nicely formed.

Now they were getting someplace, Longarm thought with pleasure.

Her bush was a dense patch of curly gold hair set on a prominent mound that already glistened in the candlelight with small droplets of eager moisture. He guessed she'd been looking forward to this damned near as much as he was if she was that wet and ready before they even got started.

Where in hell did that notion ever come from that Scandinavian women were supposed to be aloof and untouchable ice princesses?

This particular one had the looks for it but not the actions.

The hem of her nightdress crept higher.

Her waist was impossibly small above that rounded swell of shapely ass.

He wished she'd get on with it now.

She stopped where she was, smiling at him over the folds of cloth she was holding, and he rolled his eyes, suspecting that what she wanted was some expression of eagerness from him. Fine. Give it to her and let her move right along.

She drew the nightdress higher, covering her pretty face now but exposing her tits to view.

That was better.

Marta still couldn't compare with Miss Day. But she couldn't be far behind that standard of excellence either.

The girl's tits were magnificent. Large and pale and pink-tipped. Bold and firm and needing no support other than what nature already provided. By the time she reached thirty they might be hanging below her belly button. But not now. Now they stood tall and proud, lightly blue-veined beneath softly translucent skin. Their already impressive size seemed magnified all the more in comparison with her exceptionally small nipples.

Her nipples looked to be as hard as Longarm's cock was.

She pulled the nightdress the rest of the way off and dropped it onto the floor.

She gave her head a shake, and that stream of soft, golden hair shimmered in the candlelight and flowed across her chest and down her back.

Marta posed in front of him again, turning and preening under his gaze, obviously enjoying the admiration that he gave her.

She was a handsome filly and knew it and reveled in the knowledge.

She cupped her tits in her palms and lifted them as if offering them to him.

Then she dipped her head and lifted more until she was able to reach out with the tip of her tongue and slowly lick first one nipple and then the next, her eyes locked on his all the while so that she could observe his reactions. Her pink, delicate tongue circled, slowed, circled again. The touch of it left moisture catching the light and shining wherever it had been.

Longarm chuckled and wondered what was next.

Marta ran her hands down her body, caressing her own torso. Onto the flat plane of her stomach. Into the thick bush at her vee.

She touched herself there, her eyes still meeting his, and smiled as she probed inside herself with a fingertip.

She tilted her pelvis toward him and spread her legs, exposing herself to his view.

With the fingers of one hand she pulled her vaginal lips wide apart. The shade of pink flesh was darker there. Redder. Almost raw. Longarm suspected Marta had been rubbing and fingering herself, bringing herself off, while she waited for her parents to get to sleep so she could come and get the real thing.

She gave him a long look, then smiled coyly and with the other hand dipped a finger inside, then another and another.

She filled her own flesh and gasped, her eyelids drooping nearly closed at the pleasures she was extracting from her own body.

Longarm frowned just a little and peevishly wondered if Marta had come here to fuck a man or just to show off in front of one. An eager young woman was a joy. But a prick-tease was something he could comfortably live without.

Marta stood there in front of him and masturbated herself to a climax, shuddering and going limp in the knees at the end so that she staggered and had to catch herself from falling.

She sighed and smiled and stood upright again, then turned and bent over so that he could admire her ass. It was shapely, true, but not good for much if it was going to be kept at a distance.

"Is this a private party," he growled, "or did you want a game that two can play?"

"Shh."

"No, I won't shush, dammit," he whispered. "If this here is all you want, go do it in front of a mirror."

Marta looked like she was going to cry. "I thought it would please you."

"A little of it does, girl. But there's such a thing as too much of an otherwise good thing. Now what is it you're wanting t' do here?"

"I want you," she whispered, her eyes wide but definitely not innocent.

"Then come here an' show me that you do."

She padded contritely to his bedside and lay down beside him, her hand finding and fondling and teasing him. Not that he needed any more encouragement in that area.

107

She bent over him, her hair falling on either side of his head like a shimmering, golden tent. She covered his mouth with hers. Her lips were soft and mobile, and her tongue fenced with his inside the privacy of their mouths.

This was more like it, Longarm decided.

She toyed with his balls and ran her fingers up and down his shaft.

He cupped one lovely breast in his hand and squeezed gently. Her tit was so firm it felt almost hard, and her nipple in his palm was hot and sharp.

Yeah, this was definitely more like it.

Longarm pulled her down onto the bed beside him and stroked her smooth, warm flesh.

Marta gasped and shuddered.

"You didn't . . . ?"

"But I did," she whispered happily.

"I'll be damned."

"So will I." She giggled. "But I like it."

He chuckled and reached for her crotch.

His fingers found the soft, wet curls. Longarm was ready and more than ready and so, obviously, was she. He raised himself off the bed, preparing to move on top of her. Marta parted her legs and tugged at him to hurry.

"No!"

The bedroom door crashed open, and the room was filled with light as Troy Tate rushed in carrying a lamp with him.

"Damn," Longarm muttered. The irate father's timing couldn't have been much worse.

"You son of a bitch," Tate roared.

Longarm sighed and reached over to pull the sheet over himself. Apologies weren't going to help here, and he knew it. He was just going to have to sit through Tate's fussing and fuming and then go set up camp for himself for the rest of this night, damn it.

At least there was no real harm done. And Longarm figured if Tate was stupid enough to want to get physical about it, Longarm could persuade him against the idea and hopefully keep from hurting the man while he was doing it. He supposed he owed Tate that much consideration anyhow.

Marta shrieked and squirmed. She threw herself off the bed and grabbed for the discarded nightdress. She was in tears and sounded almost hysterical.

"He made me do it, Papa."

Uh, oh, Longarm thought.

"He told me to come here because he wanted to talk to me. And then . . . and then he touched me . . . and I was so scared . . . I was so scared, Papa, that I couldn't call out to you and Mama . . . he said he'd hurt me, Papa . . . he said he'd beat me if I screamed."

Longarm made a face. Thank you *so* much, Miss Marta Tate.

He could understand what the girl was doing, of course. But he couldn't much enjoy the experience.

Hell, he would just have to let things get calmed down a bit and then explain it. Damn it.

"He tried to rape me, Papa."

Tate was hugging his daughter and crying and now Maud was at the door too, grabbing at the girl and dragging her out of the room.

Every-damn-body but Longarm was crying by now, and the girl was babbling and Maud was bellowing and Troy was dithering between them and Longarm like he didn't know whether he ought to be comforting his wife and daughter or trying to punch Long.

Longarm sighed. This was just about the shits.

"Take Marta to her room, Maud. And run get Marshal Barnes."

"You do whatever you want, Tate, but are you *sure* you want the real story t' come out here?" Longarm cautioned.

"You shut up, mister. Just you shut your mouth. Maud, do what I said. Go get Marshal Barnes. We're going to charge this man with rape."

Longarm shook his head sadly and fixed Marta with a look that he hoped would tell her plain as words that he wasn't going to lie about it if her father insisted on pressing charges.

Protecting the girl's reputation was one thing, but being dumb enough to accept a criminal charge was another.

109

And in Longarm's personal book, rape—the genuine thing, that is—was about as serious as criminal charges got.

"You'd best think this through, Tate," he warned.

"What you'd best do, you son of a bitch, is to shut your mouth. We're charging you—"

"Dammit, man, the girl came in here uninvited and put on a strip show that'd make a Kansas City coochee-coochee dancer blush. And I won't be inclined to lie to the law just to save your daughter's reputation. Now you think about that before you bring anybody else into this."

"Why you son of a bitch, this child is only fifteen years old. How dare you. . . . You can't expect me to believe. . . . This innocent child is. . . . "

Longarm groaned, not even hearing the rest of that tirade.

Fifteen years old? Come *on* now.

He glared at Marta—who just *had* to be eighteen or more—but the girl was sobbing against her mother's breast and babbling denials that were lies pure and simple.

"Aw, shit," Longarm snarled. He sat upright on the side of the bed, ignoring the presence of the girl and Mrs. Tate, and began pulling his clothes on.

This night was beginning to look like a long and unpleasant one.

Chapter 23

Longarm sat with his head down and gave himself a thorough cussing. Which was what he'd been doing much of the damned night.

One good thing, though. He hadn't had to worry about a place to sleep for the remainder of the night.

The town of Beck City had been kind enough to provide that for him.

He sure did wish they'd spent the money to buy a decent-sized jail cage, though. Nobody taller than a midget could stand upright inside this steel barred thing. And he'd had to sleep curled up like a dog in a gutter.

It was as uncomfortable as it was embarrassing.

Longarm was beginning to think that criminals were even more stupid than he'd always believed, if only because so many of them got caught for their crimes more than once.

A guy would grab them and put them away and they'd serve their time, and next thing you knew they would be back out and doing the same things all over again.

Stupid.

Longarm couldn't see why a man would want to risk the repeat of an experience like this one. Once should be plenty bad enough to discourage a fellow from lawbreaking.

Criminals weren't the only ones who could be stupid, though.

Why hadn't he seen that that damn girl was underage?

Hell, she looked plenty old enough. And she acted *more* than old enough.

But there should have been *something* to tip him off to it.

At least he had to give her father some credit. Right at first there Longarm had had to wonder if the Family Tate had come up with a confidence scam to supplement their income, the three of them working together to deliberately set up a traveling stranger so they could extract a hush-money payment from him. It wasn't all that unusual a scam.

Giving credit where it was due, though, Troy Tate was sincere as hell about believing in his dear daughter's innocence.

The man was genuinely outraged. And of course he believed the lying little prick-tease's denials and tears and pleas.

Damn that little juvenile bitch anyhow. The hot-twat little slut had Custis Long by the short hairs, damn her, and wasn't about to start telling the truth now. Given the choice between his ass and her reputation—and that was exactly what this came down to—he had no doubt whatsoever about what her choice was going to be.

Longarm scowled and sighed.

Then he smiled a little.

Not that there was a single stinking thing that was funny about this situation.

It was just that he couldn't help wishing he could see the expression on Billy Vail's face when word about this got to Denver.

You've done the boss proud this time, haven't you, Longarm thought unhappily.

Sent out on a special mission for the Justice Department

112

and look what happens. Thank you very much, Mister Attorney General.

Longarm looked up in response to the sound of someone coming up the City Hall steps. Several someones. It was about time someone got around to bringing him some breakfast. Being inside a bear cage didn't completely kill a man's appetite, he was discovering.

"Good morning, Marshal."

"Keep your mouth shut," Barnes snapped.

Longarm shrugged. He had to be disappointed, though, that Marshal Barnes's hands were empty. There was no breakfast tray.

He thought about asking, then decided that if he wanted to eat anytime soon he was probably better off waiting for Barnes to think about it. Otherwise the young marshal would likely refuse to feed him just because he knew Longarm was hungry. Barnes hadn't been particularly friendly or understanding last night when Tate made his complaint. In fact, Barnes had acted like Custis Long was just about the foulest son of a bitch ever to come down the pike.

The other footsteps on the stairs continued, and the other Barnes boys, Danny and Lute, came into view. Still no tray, but one of them was carrying something wrapped in a cotton towel.

"Here." Danny came over to the cage and made a face as he shoved the small bundle against the bars.

Longarm took it from him and had to unwrap it so he could pull out the food inside piece by piece. It was only a handful of cold, stale biscuits. No butter, no jam, no coffee to go with the dry biscuits. He supposed that was better than nothing. Marginally. "Thank you," he said.

The Barnes boys ignored him.

"What do you do for trials around here?" Longarm asked.

The brothers gathered around Jeff's desk and talked softly among themselves. Longarm might as well not have spoken for all the answer he got.

"Do you intend to actually investigate the charges," Longarm persisted, "or just take Tate's word for what happened?"

113

Brick walls could have been more responsive than the Barnes boys were.

"Is any one of you three aware that in this country a man is supposed to be presumed innocent until he's proved guilty?"

Longarm clamped his jaw shut in sudden surprise.

How the hell many times had he heard that selfsame line from a prisoner of his? Damn.

He liked to think that he really and truly treated his prisoners like they were presumed innocent.

But did he? Did he really?

He sure as hell hoped he treated them better than Deputy U.S. Marshal Jeff Barnes did.

Still, this experience right here was food for thought, wasn't it?

Or should he bother?

If he couldn't find some way to get the truth out about this, Deputy U.S. Marshal Custis Long wasn't going to have to be thinking in terms of how he treated his own prisoners.

Because right soon he would not *be* Deputy U.S. Marshal Custis Long anymore, not if he couldn't get a fair hearing about his side of things.

Hell, he wouldn't even be *Mister* Custis Long if that was so.

Far as he could recall, prisoners weren't much granted the honorific title of Mister.

Longarm dropped his eyes back toward the floor of the jail cage and concentrated on cussing and mumbling, both being directed about fifty-fifty between that treacherous little hot-tail Marta Tate and the monumental stupidity of a certain Custis Long.

Chapter 24

Longarm reached for a cheroot, the unconscious action repeated now for probably the twentieth time in the past hour, then scowled and put the damn thing back into his pocket again. Marshal Jeff Barnes had been nice enough to let the prisoner keep his smokes, but had confiscated all Longarm's matches to make sure he couldn't start a fire in the jail cage.

The Barnes boys continued to sit around the desk shooting the shit and ignoring the prisoner. Longarm had long since quit trying to talk to them. They weren't interested in hearing any of it.

Their conversation stopped and all eyes, Longarm's included, shifted toward the stairway when footsteps approached from that direction.

A jaunty, neatly brushed black derby hat bobbed into view first, then the face and shoulders of banker Andy Beck, his eyeglasses catching the light and reflecting back a blank, flat glaze like a pair of small mirrors mounted on the bridge of his nose.

All three of the brothers, Longarm noticed, came to their feet as soon as they saw who the visitor was. "Good morning, sir."

Beck stopped at the head of the stairs and planted his hands on his hips. He glared about the room, taking in the brothers and then Longarm in his miserable cage.

"I suppose you heard, sir, 'bout . . . "

"Shut up, Jeff."

"Yes, sir."

The banker took another step toward the marshal's desk and first fixed Jeff with his stare, then Danny and Lute. He motioned over his shoulder with a thumb. "Out," he said.

"Sir?"

"Out, dammit. I want to talk to Long. In private."

"Yes, sir." There was a general scramble for hats.

"What did Mr. Long have for breakfast?" Beck demanded.

"Well, sir, it was, uh . . . "

"Never mind. I can guess. Go over to the cafe and get him something decent to eat. Eggs, sausage, the works. But I don't want to see any of you back up here sooner than a half hour from now. You understand me?"

"Yes, sir, but if Miz Tate knows who—"

"If they have a problem with what I want done, Jeffrey, you tell them they'll have to take it up with me. Understood?"

"Yes, sir," the deputy United States marshal for the Judith Basin meekly responded.

Longarm's eyes narrowed a little in concentration. This was a side of young Andy Beck that he hadn't suspected. No young and eager hale-fellow-well-met here. Behind the mild exterior, young Mr. Beck was hiding a core of tempered steel. And he wasn't shy about using it when he wished.

"Half an hour," Beck said. "And don't forget the sausage."

"Yes, sir." Jeff and his brothers jammed their hats onto their heads and scurried down the stairs.

Beck stood where he was, waiting until the City Hall door slammed shut again, before he turned and with a disarming smile crossed the floor to the jail cage. He reached in between the bars to offer Longarm a handshake.

"Sorry I can't stand t' greet you proper, but you know how it is," Longarm said.

Beck chuckled. "Yes, I see how it is."

"Cheap rent," Longarm observed. "Reckon there's always something a fella can be grateful for."

The banker threw his head back and laughed. "Excuse me for a moment, Mr. Long. Uh, don't go away."

Longarm grinned and squatted in a front corner of the tiny cell.

Beck dropped his derby onto Jeff Barnes's desk, then dragged a chair over to the cell so he could sit more or less at Longarm's eye level.

"I am familiar with the charge against you, of course," Beck said.

"Are we finally getting to the stage when someone is willing to listen to my denials?"

"That is what I came to hear, Mr. Long. And I don't mind telling you that I am, to be perfectly frank, predisposed in your favor, sir." He smiled. "Loretta made that quite clear over breakfast this morning, you see. After her own frightening experiences on that riverboat she is adamant that you are not the sort of man who could ever do a thing like that. Very much to the contrary, she insists. So you do have at least one friend at court."

"I can't say as I'm real disappointed to hear that, Mr. Beck. You wouldn't have a match by any chance, would you?"

Beck fished a box of them out of his pocket, declined the offer of a cheroot, and waited until Longarm had his first smoke of the day lighted before he went on.

"Mmm, that does ease the pain," Longarm said pleasantly as he exhaled a smoke ring into the air between them. "Thanks."

"My pleasure. Now, sir. What can you tell me about last night?"

Longarm shrugged. "To tell you the truth, Mr. Beck . . . "

"Andy. Please."

"All right. Andy. To tell you the truth, Andy, my first

117

thought was that it was a setup. A clumsy blackmail attempt."

Beck nodded. "I am familiar with the scam," he said.

"So'm I, and that's what I thought was happening. But those poor folks Troy and Maud are serious. They really believe I was trying to seduce their daughter. Who I think you will admit sure as hell doesn't look her age."

"I have no argument with that statement, Mr. Long."

"Custis will do, Andy."

Beck smiled again. "Custis it shall be, then."

"Anyhow . . . " Longarm explained the situation in as much detail as he felt comfortable giving. He did not want to compromise a hot-blooded and horny girl who was too young to know better. But he didn't want to sit in this cage any longer either, dammit.

Beck frowned and pursed his lips and now and then nodded with sympathetic understanding as Longarm related the sequence of events. "I see," he said finally.

"Sounds farfetched, prob'ly," Longarm said at length. "But it happens t' be so. The Tates are sincere in what they told everyone. They just don't happen t' know quite all they think they do."

"Not so farfetched as you might think at the moment," Beck agreed. "I don't know if you are aware of this, Custis, but bankers tend to hear the most intimate things from people. Perhaps even more so than doctors and barbers."

"Really?" Longarm didn't know where that comment was leading, but he was willing to listen to whatever it was. Besides, he hadn't anything better to do at the moment.

"As an example . . . can I trust you to maintain a confidence, Custis?"

Longarm grinned. "I can promise you true and absolute that I will not run down into the street and spread a word of it."

Beck laughed. "Right. Well, Custis, the plain truth is that I happen to know that the Tate family removed from their recent home in the wake of a scandal."

"Oh?"

"It wouldn't be appropriate for me to go into details, you

118

understand, so suffice it to say that the scandal involved the girl Marta and a, um, male companion of considerably advanced age."

"Damn." It made sense, though. Based both on the few things Troy Tate had said in conversation and, more, the things Longarm had personally seen last night. "Damn," he repeated.

"My problem," Beck went on, "is not my belief in your innocence, Custis. You already have that. The problem as I see it, really, is to find some justification for clearing your name here while trying to maintain some facade of innocence for that girl."

Longarm frowned. He could see that as a problem, sure, but . . .

"Troy and Maud are good people, Custis. Decent, honest, very hard-working. They are an asset to the community, and I shouldn't want to lose them. You see, Custis, I am trying to build for the future here. I want a solid citizenry. And I would like to maintain a public front that will allow the Tates to continue here." He smiled. "And of course I must satisfy Loretta's demands that you be released without delay."

It was Longarm's turn to smile. It seemed that Banker Beck was willing to crack the whip over the law in Beck City. But that Miss Day was the one who did all the whip-cracking at home.

"Is there anything you can tell me, Custis, that would, um, expedite your acceptance as the victim of an innocent misunderstanding?" Andy Beck leaned forward with his hands clasped together, his expression all helpfulness and concern.

Longarm sighed. Maybe . . .

"You asked me t' keep a confidence, Andy, an' I'll do it. Now I'll give you one that you may or may not be able t' keep."

"Yes?"

"I been passing around the story here that I'm a cowman outa Denver looking for new graze."

"Yes."

"Well, you see, Andy, the truth is . . . "

Chapter 25

"Keys," Beck demanded as Marshal Barnes and his brothers came back up the stairs, Jeff in the lead with Danny behind him and Lute bringing up the rear with a loaded breakfast tray.

"What?"

"You heard me, Jeff. Get your keys and let this gentleman out."

"But . . ."

"*Do* it!"

"Yes, sir." Jeff plainly did not like what he was being told. But he jumped to do it anyway.

While Jeff was busy finding his jail keys in the depths of a cluttered drawer, Andy Beck was just as busy ordering Danny and Lute away. "Leave that on the desk, Lute, and both of you disappear. You should have better things to do than sit around here anyhow. Go do some of them. And while you're at it, find Abner and tell him that I want to see him this afternoon. Over lunch, say."

"Yes, sir," Danny said quickly. If this had been a military outfit he and his brother, Longarm saw, would've snapped rigidly to attention and saluted. As it was, they squared their shoulders and their jaws and did their best to look attentive and obedient. When Andy Beck spoke, these boys moved on the double-quick.

Lute put Longarm's breakfast tray down on the marshal's desk, then he and Danny hurried down the stairs without a backward glance toward Jeff.

Jeff fumbled with the padlock key but finally got the cage door open. Longarm picked up his Stetson, and had to hunch over even lower to get through the low doorway. It felt damned good to be able to stand fully upright and stretch for a change. Jeff stood back eyeing the now–non-prisoner with suspicion, the fingers of one hand toying with the butt of the Colt on his belt as if he expected Longarm to make a break for it now that he was out of the cell.

"Jeffrey, I want you to meet Deputy United States Marshal Custis Long," Andy Beck said.

Barnes blinked. "What the . . . ?"

"It's true, Jeff. He showed me his credentials. Which you somehow managed to miss finding, assuming you remembered to search your prisoner at all before you locked him away."

"But . . . "

"Are you listening to me, Jeff?"

"Yes, sir, Mr. Beck." The confused young marshal scowled but held his curiosity reluctantly in check.

"Deputy Long has explained his mission here, Jeff, and it is not in conflict with the duties of your office. He is here on the trail of a criminal wanted in Colorado. A man named Ambrose Warren. Marshal Vail there received a tip that this Warren fellow may be in the Judith Basin, and Marshal Vail was not aware that you already held a deputy's appointment here. He dispatched Deputy Long undercover, as it were, to find Warren and arrest him."

Longarm had shared a confidence with Andy Beck. But he hadn't told him *every*thing. He hadn't mentioned anything, for instance, about Marshal Hall or the suspicions

121

that had been attached to him, and therefore by inference to Deputy Barnes as well. Longarm certainly hadn't wanted to say anything about the political implications of the situation. Besides, at this point all of that looked to be so much hot air anyhow. Better not to raise unfounded rumors unless there looked to be some basis for them.

"You are not to tell anyone else about this, Jeff. Not even Danny and Lute. I promised Custis that we would maintain his cover story if at all possible, and that is exactly what we will try to do. We've agreed to a story explaining last night's, um, misunderstanding."

"But everybody in town already—"

"You aren't listening to me, Jeffrey."

"Sorry."

"What happened last night, Jeff, is that Custis and Miss Tate both got up in the night and left their rooms to use the facilities. They bumped into each other in the corridor. Custis thought Miss Tate was falling and therefore tried to help her by grasping her about the waist. Miss Tate, half asleep, misunderstood his gentlemanly assistance. She honestly but mistakenly believed she was being attacked. She screamed. Her parents ran to rescue her. In the confusion and the emotions of the moment, no one listened to Mr. Long's explanations. Until this morning. This morning, Jeff, *you* heard the true facts and immediately acted to correct an unfortunate situation. Is that clear, Jeff?"

"But everybody in town already knows what—"

"Jeffrey," Beck said in a sad, patient tone.

"Yes, sir?"

"Lie, Jeffrey. Stand right there and lie through your teeth, um? Repeat the story often enough and strongly enough, Jeffrey, and before nightfall tonight everyone will believe this story just as readily as they believed the first. Custis and the young lady bumped into each other in the dark. The rest of it was all misunderstanding."

"I reckon we can get the townspeople t' buy that, sir, but what about Mister and Miz Tate themselves?" It was a reasonable question, Longarm conceded.

122

"When I leave here, Jeff, I will go have a talk with them. I can assure you that the Tate family, all of them, will fully support this story."

"Yes, sir," Jeff said.

"And remember now, no one is to learn about Deputy Long's real purpose here."

"Yes, sir."

Beck smiled and took Longarm by the elbow, leading him to the desk where the breakfast tray sat leaking tantalizing aromas into the room. "I think you'll find the sausage particularly good," he was saying. "One of the farmers here, a gentleman of German descent, has a knack for making the finest sausage I've ever tasted. I insist on having his sausages on my own table every morning. I know you will enjoy them."

Longarm was interested in the food, all right, dang near any kind of it after those dry and tasteless biscuits, but first he hauled open the desk drawer where he'd seen Jeff Barnes put his gunbelt with the big Colt Thunderer. He wouldn't feel right again until that was in place.

Not that he'd been completely weaponless, even when he was inside that jail cell. Marshal Barnes's shakedown had been an inexpert affair, and the Beck City lawman hadn't discovered the little hideout derringer that rode on the end of Longarm's watch chain. Not that the small gun would have been any help to him in there anyway. Longarm hadn't had any intentions of gunning down a fellow deputy regardless of circumstances, and simply hadn't given any thought to the presence of the derringer in his vest. Didn't see any reason to bring it up to Barnes now either, for that matter.

He strapped the familiar weight of the double-action Colt back at his waist where it belonged, Barnes eyeing him unhappily while he did so, and then sat down to breakfast at Jeff Barnes's desk.

"Take your time, Custis," Andy Beck said. "By the time you're finished eating, I'll have talked to the Tates." He smiled. "And don't forget tonight. Loretta and I shall be expecting you for dinner."

"Thanks, Andy."

123

"My pleasure, Custis. Truly." The banker picked up his derby and perched it atop his head, then went cheerfully down the stairs to see the Tates.

Longarm thoroughly enjoyed his meal even if he did have to do so in silence. Marshal Jeff Barnes didn't seem much interested in being companionable at the moment.

Chapter 26

Longarm felt a helluva lot better when he stepped out into the sweet, pure air of freedom.

He stood outside the City Hall door and filled his lungs and lifted his face to the bright, pale, buttermilk sky.

Funny how such simple things can please after so short a time without the freedom of movement that folks take for granted every day of their lives. Longarm was no exception to that.

He stood there at the side of the street and just plain enjoyed being able to stand in the sunshine there on the side of the street.

This beat any kind of jail cell, and in particular the bear cage owned by the town of Beck City, Montana Territory.

The sense of well-being filled him from scalp to toenails. His belly was warm and full—Andy Beck had been right about that German's sausage—and he was free to go on about his business.

He would still have to face the Tate family, of course. All his things were still in the room behind their cafe. But he would worry about that, and about another place to sleep while he was here, later on.

One thing he was sure of was that he wasn't again going to try sleeping under the same roof as that treacherous little bitch Marta. Beck was trying to be considerate of her folks, and that was fine. But Longarm figured there was something seriously wrong with the girl, and he didn't want her to have another crack at his bedroom door. If for no other reason than because his balls were still aching from getting all that worked up and then being left hanging.

He had no regrets about not finishing what the girl had started. He didn't want to find himself messing with a half-crazy, overdeveloped child even if it was unknowingly. But he couldn't help wishing the incident hadn't ever gotten started to begin with. The frustrations of being left like that were damn near as bad as the night in the cage had been.

He glanced down the street in the general direction of Clete Miller's smithy, and wondered if he would accomplish more toward finding Ambrose Warren by riding out and talking to the farmers in the countryside or if he should hang around town and talk to the merchants.

Barnes, with poor grace and a grudging willingness, had given him more details about the recent spate of robberies in the area, so at least now Longarm had more to work with in his search.

Start at the beginning and work from there, Longarm decided. Start with Warren's victims.

He turned toward the smithy, where his horse was being kept.

"My God, lookee there!" someone shouted.

"It's him. He's escaped."

"Grab your guns, boys, the rapist's on the loose."

Oh, shit, Longarm thought.

There weren't very many men in town in the middle of a working day, but everyone who was available came charging out into the street. Better than half of them were

126

carrying one sort of weapon or another.

"Whoa, boys," Longarm called. "Don't nobody get excited."

A wild-eyed man with shaving lather covering half his face and a sheet draped over his chest came running out of the barber's with an antique pepperbox cap-and-ball pistol in his hand. The barber was right behind him waving a straight razor. Others who were hurrying into view held an assortment of rifles and shotguns. One damn fool actually came running out with a sword.

"Now dammit, hold on here," Longarm insisted.

He held his hands well away from the Colt at his waist and shouted over his shoulder for Barnes to come down and tell these idiots to back off.

All the available firepower in Beck City seemed to be pointing down Longarm's throat at the moment.

"Don't shoot," he called.

There was no sign of Jeff Barnes, but across the way at the Tate store Andy Beck appeared and came running over, Troy and Maud Tate both right behind him.

"Hold it. Everybody just hold it," the banker ordered.

No one looked particularly pleased. But at least no one was shooting yet either.

"Hold on there, I said. John, put that thing down before you hurt somebody. Lou, you too. Charley, Ben. All of you quit this, hear?"

Maud Tate hung back out of the line of possible fire while Beck and her husband rushed over to Longarm's side. Troy Tate, Longarm noticed, arrived puffing and out of breath. Andy Beck might just have gotten up from an armchair for all the exertion showing in his breathing.

"What the hell is this, Mr. Beck?" someone demanded.

"Yeah, Mr. Beck. Why is this fiend loose again?"

"Everybody put your guns down and come closer here," Beck told them. "It's probably a good thing that this is happening, boys. Now you can hear it from Mr. Tate himself. Troy, you tell them."

Tate flushed a deep, rich shade of red with the embarrassment of it.

But Andy Beck had persuaded the man to accept and spread the agreed-upon fiction, and Tate did it.

In a low but clear voice he told all his fellow townspeople that no, there hadn't been any attempted rape of young Marta last night. It was all a regrettable misunderstanding. Mr. Long was innocent of any wrongdoing and so was the girl.

Tate dutifully reported the whopper that Andy Beck and Longarm had come up with in the jail.

As for the many parts of the story that couldn't begin to fit the facts—transplanting the incident, for instance, out of a storeroom that existed and into a hallway that didn't, or trying to explain why either party would be going to the outhouse in the middle of the night when there were thunder mugs right there handy, or getting into the questions of Marta's state of undress—all that was glossed over and ignored.

No one who was listening asked any questions.

But then of course why should they, when it was the girl's own aggrieved father who was providing the explanations and the town's leading citizen who was standing right there agreeing with him?

Like Beck had already said, Longarm conceded, it probably worked out just fine this way. A stranger's explanation would be suspect, but Troy Tate and Andy Beck these folks pretty much had to believe.

Maud Tate stayed out in the middle of the street. Longarm glanced in her direction once. The woman's expression was one of sheer disgust.

With her husband for going along with the fabrication? With Longarm for standing here a free man now? Least likely, he supposed, with Marta, who was the real root of the problem.

Likely Longarm never would know where Maud Tate's true feelings on the subject lay.

Likely that was just as well anyhow.

One thing for sure, though. Longarm was doubly glad now that he wouldn't have to stay again under the same roof as the Tate family. Right now he thought Maud looked near about as murderous as last night her daughter had looked seductive.

The crowd of men frowned in concentration for a while as they listened. Then soon enough the weapons were lowered and a few sheepish expressions began to show here and there.

The man with the sword looked down at it, then at the big Colt at Longarm's waist. The sword-bearer blanched, probably realizing for the first time the futility of opposing gunpowder with naked steel.

Most of the men waited until all the explanations were in, then shuffled forward to mumble apologies before they turned back to the pursuit of their own affairs.

Longarm was damned glad that was over and done with. At least now he could walk the streets in safety, without having to worry about people mistaking him for an escaped felon and potting him out of a sense of public-spiritedness.

Hell, getting shot by a criminal in the line of duty would be bad enough. But to be shot by a well-meaning citizen would be by-damn humiliating.

"No harm done, boys," he told them graciously. "All over with now."

Andy Beck chuckled and gave Longarm a wink that the others couldn't see as the crowd took their weapons and dispersed.

Troy Tate lingered behind a few moments more. The man gave Longarm an embarrassed look—Longarm guessed that Tate was willing to be realistic about his daughter's problems even if Maud wasn't yet—then turned and took his wife by the elbow to lead her back to the store.

"Reckon I owe you my thanks again, Andy."

"My pleasure, Custis. See you for dinner tonight." Beck headed off toward his bank, and Longarm walked down the street unmolested to Miller's smithy.

He was about halfway there when it occurred to him that Marshal Jeff Barnes never had come down those stairs to make any explanations or to offer any sort of protection to his fellow deputy U.S. marshal.

Surely the youngster couldn't feel so insecure about himself that he was willing to let another peace officer be shot down in the street just so the two of them wouldn't be in competition here.

On the other hand, surely the young SOB couldn't be so deaf as to not have heard what was going on right underneath his office window.

Longarm decided it might not be a good idea to count too heavily on Jeff Barnes if he needed any help in the future.

He grimaced and reached for a cheroot.

Chapter 27

Longarm ducked to pass underneath the lintel into the smithy. The rough, driftwood timber of the lintel and the roof beams above were about all the wood that had been used in the construction of the sod structure.

Clete Miller's forge was hot, the coals glowing a bright, just-stoked red, but there was no sign of the smith there.

"Clete?"

Longarm sensed a presence at his side and a flicker of motion.

He darted backward, his hand automatically sweeping the big Colt out of his holster even as he fell and rolled, coming onto his feet again in a crouch with the Colt extended and searching for a target.

A lethal chunk of something whistled through the air where Longarm's head had just been, but the blow failed to connect.

The force of it and the weight of the object pulled Longarm's attacker off balance and into view in the doorway.

Longarm shook his head and stood upright. He shoved the Thunderer back into the cross-draw holster.

"Damn it, Clete, leave be."

Miller eyed first Longarm and then the gun that Longarm had just put away. He bent and retrieved the billet of unworked iron he'd just tried to brain Longarm with, and hefted it.

"You weren't down at City Hall just now, Clete, or you'd have heard."

"Heard what?" the smith asked suspiciously.

"About the misunderstanding last night."

The smith's eyes narrowed, but at least he was willing to listen. The fact that Longarm hadn't chosen to shoot him just now—but still could take a notion to—probably had something to do with that.

"Misunderstanding?"

Longarm gave him the phony but useful story, and Miller visibly relaxed.

"Sorry 'bout that, Custis," he said with a weak smile. Then the expression strengthened and turned into a grin. "I dunno, Custis, this kinda thing keeps up, you're likely to get a bad impression about the folks around here. Yesterday we're thinking you're a robber. Last night we're calling you a rapist. Kinda glad now that you wasn't drug out and hung last night."

It was the first Longarm had heard about that idea. Late-night whiskey talk, more than likely. "I'm kinda glad too that I wasn't," he agreed.

Miller grinned again. "Maybe even more'n me, huh?"

"It's a possibility," Longarm said.

"Yeah, I bet. So, uh, what can I do for you by way of apology?"

"Two things, actually. One, I wanted to collect my horse and take a swing around the country."

"Glad to hear you're still thinking of settling here, Custis," Miller said, although of course that wasn't Longarm's intention at all.

"The other thing, Clete, I was wondering if I could bunk on your hay or some such accommodation while I'm here.

132

I'd pay you room rent, of course. But I think you can understand how I wouldn't want to stay with the Tates anymore. Be kinda awkward for everybody."

"Sure." The blacksmith rubbed his chin—he hadn't taken time yet to go into town and get a shave, and it showed—then said, "I could put you in a corner of the shop here. No room in the shed, and besides, I can see that you're a smoker. Best if you don't sleep on my hay. But I'd be glad to let you throw your roll inside the place here."

"That sounds fine."

"No extra charge over what you're already paying for the horse. No extra trouble either. Hell, I expect that's the least us Beck Citians can do to make you feel welcome for a change."

"I appreciate that, Clete."

"No problem." The smith turned back to his forge. After being untended for these few minutes the coals were already showing a dull gray instead of the bright, cherry red they had been when Longarm first tried to walk inside.

Miller picked up a pair of heavy tongs, lifting them as easily as if they were made of cork instead of steel, and began rearranging some bits of iron that were heating in the coals. A hay rake with two broken tines sat on the shop floor nearby.

Longarm helped out by grabbing the bellows handles and starting to pump them, building the heat back up to where it would have to be for a weld.

"Why, thank you, Custis."

"No problem. Oh, say, Clete, while I think about it, I heard somewhere that a fella I used to know might be up in this country now. Maybe you know him."

As if it were the most casual and unimportant question possible, Longarm began to give Clete Miller a description of Ambrose Warren.

It was time, he figured, that he got down to work here. Time to quit allowing himself to be the prey and concentrate on being the predator that he naturally was.

Chapter 28

"Thank you, ma'am." Longarm touched the brim of his Stetson, then nodded to the lady's husband. "And thank you, Sam. I appreciate your suggestions." He reined the horse away and started slowly toward the farmyard gate, the young roan shuffling through a flock of scrawny chickens without spooking at the unaccustomed creatures.

The farmer and his wife were friendly. Or at least had proven to be once their first fears eased. Strangers riding in the Judith right now were initially suspect, but the Markhams were pleasant, decent, outgoing folk who quickly warmed to their visitor and answered all his questions freely. Not helpfully, it was true, but freely.

The process of looking for Ambrose Warren in this fashion was going to take some time, he could see now. Perhaps it had been a mistake to come here under pretense, but that was the way Billy Vail thought it best.

As it was, though, posing as a cattleman in search of grass, Longarm had to waste his time on endless questions about rainfall and growing seasons and land prices.

It would've been easier if he simply could have ridden in, flashed his badge, and told people he was looking for a murdering son of a bitch.

Easier, he admitted, but not necessarily more productive. Even SOBs like Warren had friends, and a fella never knew which John Citizen might be one of them.

He left the Markham farm and loped to the next farm in sight, prepared to start his slow questioning all over again. His belly sloshed and rumbled with the motion of the roan. That was from all the coffee he'd been given at the farms already visited. Although a body would think the coffee would have been sopped up and absorbed by all the pie and doughnuts and slabs of cake the farm wives pressed upon him when he stopped. He belched as he rode into the next yard, and hoped the people here wouldn't prove to be so damned polite and hospitable.

"Hello. Hello?" He sat in his saddle and waited for an invitation so he could dismount.

All the farms he'd visited so far were very much the same. Young and barely started, the sod houses finished and a scattering of sheds and lesser outbuildings. But nothing really permanent or finished yet. The men were still devoting most of their attention to the fields where the success or failure of the crops would make the difference between pay and bust.

Most of the places had draft stock and laying hens. A good many had hog pens. Very few could afford the effort and the hay for dairy or beef cows, though. Those would come eventually but not now.

"Hello," Longarm repeated.

He stood in his stirrups and looked across the fields adjacent to this place. He could see no one working there, but the corral and the wagon shed were both empty. Nobody home, he figured, and turned the roan toward the gate.

"What is it you want, mister?"

He swung back toward the low doorway leading into a soddy that was dug half its height into the earth. "Ma'am," he said politely.

The woman remained inside the soddy and peeped around the door frame with a questioning look. She was in her thirties, he judged, and poorly dressed. Other than that he couldn't much see as she was standing in deep shadow while he sat in the full glare of the afternoon sun.

"I asked what it is you want here."

"Conversation, ma'am."

"You ain't come to rob and pillage?"

A smile flickered briefly and quickly faded. He didn't want to offend her. That wasn't exactly a sensible question, though.

"No, ma'am," he assured her.

"You can step down then if you like."

"Thank you, ma'am." He dismounted and tied the roan to a nearby rail.

"Tall one, ain't you?" she said when he came closer. "Come in if you like." He had to bend low to get through the doorway, but once inside he found the floor had been dug deep enough to make the ceiling height bearable. He removed his hat and stood awkwardly in the middle of the squat, squalid little home.

Soddies can be fixed up on the inside so that they are as nice as any house. This one hadn't been. Longarm couldn't decide from just looking if the couple didn't know any better. Or if they didn't care.

Their bed was a pallet of blanket-covered straw in one corner of the single room. A bed/crib arrangement had been pegged into another corner, and a filthy-faced toddler of two or thereabouts peered over the top of its confinement. The rude crib reminded Longarm of the jail cage in Beck City.

There was no stove in the place. A mud fireplace had been built up against the back wall and a slab of stone put down for a hearth, but the top of the fireplace fed in a vague sort of way toward a hole in the ceiling. There was no chimney or pipe to hold the smoke out of the room.

Instead of a table there was half of an old wagon box upended in the middle of the floor and two crates set beside it for chairs.

"Set down if you like, mister. You want some water t' drink?"

"No thank you, ma'am, I'm fine. Is, uh, your husband at home?"

"Nope. My fool sister sent us some cash money. Herb's gone off t' likker up with it. He won't be back till he's broke again."

"I see." The woman, oddly, didn't seem at all put out by that idea. Maybe that was the behavior she saw as normal and appropriate for the head of a family.

"You said you wanted t' talk, mister?"

"I . . . maybe I should come back some other time, ma'am," Longarm suggested. "When your husband is at home, that is."

The woman opened her mouth to say something, but was interrupted by a loud and sudden wailing from the baby. She made a face and walked over to pick it up and swing it onto her hip. The child was naked and could have used a bath. It was a girl.

Old as the kid was, at least two, it immediately began pawing at its mother's breast. Without so much as bothering to look down, the slatternly woman tugged the front of her dress open and swung the child to a distended purple nipple.

Longarm blinked and looked away.

"Ha! That excite you does it, mister?"

"Ma'am?"

"I said does the sight of that titty get you worked up?"

"Uh, no, ma'am."

"You sure, mister?"

"I'm sure."

"I told you my Herb won't be back till the money runs out an' his hangover leaves be. I'll fuck you if you want. Fifty cents. Just wait till I finish feeding Nellie here. She won't be long." She cackled. "You can have whatever milk she don't take. Good for you. Strengthens a man t' take milk from a good woman's titty."

Longarm felt a burning in his ears. He was already turned away from the sight of the woman with her too-old child nursing at a sagging dug.

137

He didn't wait around even long enough to answer.

He beat a hasty, long-legged retreat for the door and the fresh air outside, and never looked back as he broke into a trot and headed for his roan.

Woman troubles and misunderstandings surrounding them he had enough of around here already, thank you.

He put the horse into a run before it ever reached the tumbledown gate, and wasn't sure—but really didn't care anyhow—if it was laughter he could hear at his back as he got the hell *out* of there.

Probably, he decided as he rode in a hurry on toward the next farm, that crazy damned woman back there didn't know Ambrose Warren anyway.

Chapter 29

Longarm rapped lightly on the front door of the Beck home. He regretted now that he'd agreed to come. The process of talking to the farmers in the vicinity of Beck City was proving to be a time-consuming one, and he resented having to quit and ride back to town so early. But he had promised. And he certainly owed Andy Beck and Loretta Day some consideration.

He flipped the stub of a cheroot into the neat but struggling bed of plantings that had been set along the front of the porch, and was smiling politely when the door was opened.

"Miss Day, nice to see you again."

"Mr. Long, so kind of you to come."

The young woman looked radiant and at ease in this setting. Longarm knew little about ladies' fashions, but even he could see that her gown was as expensive as it was elegant. It was a cloud-soft thing of robin's-egg blue cut low enough to emphasize attributes that hardly needed emphasis.

Once long ago Longarm had seen an artillery spotter's observation balloon floating at the end of its cable tethers high in the air near the Rappahannock River. The aerial device had looked something like a monumentally huge and soft sausage. Now he found himself looking at a pair of them. Except these massive balloons were warm and fleshy and firmly attached to the chest of Andy Beck's intended. Miss Day seemed blithely unaware of the effect such a display might have.

Longarm reminded himself firmly to keep his eyes locked on hers, dammit, and smiled and smiled and suffered from the strain of having to not look down.

"Come in, Mr. Long, please."

The Beck City banker was waiting in the formal parlor. He acted as proud of Loretta as if he'd designed and built her himself.

The conversation before dinner was genial and generalized, and after a suitable interval the party transferred into the dining room, where a long table had been set as if for an occasion of state.

Longarm was impressed, he supposed, but he would have preferred to be out in the countryside accomplishing something.

Still, it was hardly painful to suffer through roast duckling in orange sauce and a half-dozen other courses. The service was efficient and unobstrusive.

Miss Day handled the chores of directing the talk, most of which centered on her impending wedding ceremony. Her fiancé Mr. Beck was bringing a preacher and contingent of musicians down from Great Falls. No, there would be no family gathering; neither she nor her fiancé Mr. Beck had family with whom they could celebrate. But they had each other—smile, smile—and it would be lovely if Mr. Long could attend too; they would be *so* delighted to have him there. The ceremony would take place in three weeks come Saturday.

Andy Beck didn't look the least bit bored by all of this, and Longarm didn't show that he was. He smiled; Andy smiled; Miss Day prattled happily.

Later the happy young woman excused herself and delicately withdrew while Beck took Longarm into the study for brandy and cigars.

Longarm was no fancier of brandy. But he had to admit that Andy Beck knew a fine cigar. Longarm hadn't had better more than once or twice in his life.

"Are you having any success with your investigation, Deputy?" Beck asked when they were alone.

"Not yet," Longarm admitted.

"I must confess something to you, Long. I keep no secrets from Loretta. She knows your purpose here and your job, but she is also aware of your desire that the secret be maintained. I assure you she will tell no one."

Longarm nodded. He really hadn't expected anything else, and knew in any event that there was no such thing as a secret that was shared. Once he opened his mouth in that jail, the word was going to start spreading. The only real question was how far and how fast it would travel, not whether it would rove. Beck and Marshal Barnes and Miss Day knew for sure. Probably by now the other Barnes brothers did too. And whoever else those three might have told. It couldn't be helped.

"No harm done," Longarm said. He took a polite if uninterested sip of the brandy. There was whiskey in the decanters on Beck's bar, but that wasn't what had been offered.

"I wish I could help you in some way," Beck went on. "As I told you before, a banker hears more than people realize. But I know of no one in this area by the name of Warren." He frowned. Paused. "You know, Deputy, now that I think about it, that isn't quite correct. I do know a man named Warren. But it is his first name, not his last. Warren Adamson." He shook his head. "But that Warren couldn't be your man. He's a harmless old fellow. Something of a recluse. Lives by himself out on the prairie doing God knows what out there. I don't know him well because he doesn't do any banking."

"What does this Adamson look like?" Longarm asked as a matter of course.

"Let me see now." Beck steepled his fingertips together, thought carefully for a moment . . . then described Ambrose Warren to perfection.

Longarm sat upright in the deep armchair, the brandy and even that exceptional cigar completely forgotten for the moment. "Tell me where I can find this fella," he said sharply, his manners forgotten now too.

Chapter 30

It was late. But then you don't go looking to catch a rat in its nest and expect to do it at your convenience.

Longarm hurried back to the smithy and saddled the roan again. The horse hadn't been used hard during the day, and had had several hours to rest since Longarm brought it back to Clete Miller's pen.

He slid his Winchester into the scabbard and swung into the saddle. There was no sign of Miller at the smithy at this hour. Up the street the town was dark and silent save for a few windows showing lamplight. Even the saloons seemed to have closed down already.

The directions Andy Beck had given were imprecise but should be good enough.

Longarm rode out past the town whorehouse—it too was already dark and silent, the local population apparently getting their play in early so they would be able to rise and get to work by the dawning—and out onto the shortgrass plain.

Dogs barked and a few guinea fowl shrieked warnings as he passed by the farms. Then the sounds of civilization fell behind and there was nothing in front of him and the roan for a hundred miles or more. Nothing except grass and wind . . . and maybe Ambrose Warren.

There was no path to follow, and in this bleak country no natural landmarks to guide oneself by. The basin—Longarm thought it should have been called a dome, not a basin—was flat and featureless. He could see the few lights of Beck City behind him for miles, until the dim glow sank beneath the dark line that marked the horizon. Then Longarm might have been the only human on the face of the earth for all he could see or feel.

His sense of direction was good, though, and years of experience had taught him to judge distance as well. Fourteen, perhaps fifteen miles, the banker had said.

Longarm took the roan out a dozen miles at a swift jog, then slowed to a walk and began seriously looking for a dark bump on the horizon that would mark the site of Warren Adamson's soddy.

It turned out that he smelled it long before he was able to see it.

Chance took him downwind from the place, and a faint whiff of smoke-smell told him there was something human nearby.

He turned the roan's face into the light northerly breeze and slowed even more so he would make as little noise as possible when he approached the place.

Another mile and he could make out the faint, black-against-charcoal lump that almost certainly would be the place Andy Beck told him about. It was less than a mile in front of him.

He rode within a half mile, then dismounted and picketed the roan on the grass. He took the Winchester out of the scabbard and by habit checked the chamber to make sure there was a cartridge seated, then began a slow and patient upwind stalk.

There was no moon yet. Longarm was in no hurry. If he

144

felt he needed more light he could always wait for the moon to rise. If not . . .

This soddy was different from the farmhouses he had spent most of the day visiting.

Here there were no sheds, no draft animals and pieces of farm equipment sitting idle in the yard. Here, in fact, there was no farmyard. Just the low-roofed sod house and close to it a sod-walled pen big enough to hold a horse or two overnight.

There were no dogs or chickens or other farm animals, and if Warren Adamson had broken ground and planted a crop, Longarm neither saw the signs of it nor felt it underfoot. The ground in all directions seemed to be virgin grass undisturbed for a thousand years or more.

No people seemed to be moving either.

Longarm made a wide circuit around the place, then repeated his swing closer in.

A scrap of moon was coming into view to the east now, giving him a little more light to work by.

He could see where the sod had been taken for the building of the house. Bumps in the exposed soil there hinted that a garden had been planted where the construction sod was removed, but no commercial crop was being made and there was no sign of so much as a moldboard plow near the soddy.

There wasn't even an outhouse near the place, although a cat hole had been dug and a makeshift bench put over it for convenience. This Warren Adamson, Longarm decided, must be one rough and rugged son of a bitch—or an extra lazy one—if he was willing to put up with that arrangement through the winter months. An unshielded rig like that could give a fella frostbite in record-setting places.

Longarm soft-footed through the night with his Winchester held at the ready, drawing a little closer to the soddy and closer again.

He heard nothing inside the soddy itself. In the pen a burro lifted its head and smelled of him without complaint. No horse, not even a mule there, just the burro. The patient little desert canary seemed out of place here somehow.

Longarm investigated the pen first—he'd known of more than one good man to make the mistake of thinking a house is the only place where you will find humans and take a bullet in the back for his error—but only the burro was in there.

He took a deep breath and moved in close to the walls of the soddy itself.

A tangle of empty fur racks hung on a peg driven into the front wall. More racks, these with coyote skins stretched over them to dry, were hung along the north wall where they could air dry without being in direct sunlight.

Adamson, it seemed, was a wolfer as well as a recluse. Farmers new from the East likely wouldn't understand or appreciate that lonely occupation. Nor was there any real need for it in farm country. Wolfers generally followed the development of ranching lands and collected bounty money from cattlemen on top of whatever they got from the sale of the furs they took. Warren Adamson, or Ambrose Warren, wasn't following that normal pattern.

But then Ambrose Warren wouldn't be, would he? If this was Ambrose Warren's place, the wolfing trade would be no more than a cover story to let him come and go without suspicion.

Longarm stood against the south wall of the soddy and sniffed.

There was a chimney of sorts, a ragged thing made of small sod chunks, at the back of the house. But that wasn't where the smoke was coming from. Longarm wasn't sure, but he thought the smoke was seeping out around the eaves of the sod house itself instead of rising from the chimney. Odd if true.

He stood there silently and concentrated on listening. Nothing.

He could hear no movement inside. No snores or sighs or soft, sleeper's breath.

The only sound he could hear at all was the occasional shifting of the burro in its pen.

If anyone was inside . . . dammit, if Ambrose Warren was in there, Longarm wanted to take him.

But if it was some innocent hermit named Adamson . . .

Longarm ghosted quietly around to the front and stood beside the low door.

There was no solid door, and indeed no wooden frame to hang one from. Pegs had been driven into the sod above a lintel that looked suspiciously like the bars of an old pack saddle, and half a green buffalo hide had been hung from them to more or less block the wind. The door was placed on the east side of the soddy where it would catch the morning light and be least vulnerable to the cold winds of winter.

That was an old trick. A trapper's trick learned a generation or more ago from the native Indians. Longarm wondered if a man like Ambrose Warren would know of it.

Now he wished the moon wasn't up yet. If he pulled the buffalo robe aside and went through that door he would be silhouetted against the night sky.

If he waited . . . if he waited, no harm would be done, he realized. If anyone was sleeping inside the soddy, they would have to waken and come out sometime. If anyone came back to it in the night, Longarm would be there waiting for them.

He went back around to the south side of the soddy and sat there with the Winchester across his lap and his back leaning comfortably against the sun-warmed wall.

He pulled out a cheroot, lighted it, and settled in to wait. The wind was coming from the north, so the smoke from his cigar would drift away from the soddy and no harm would be done. Otherwise he would have gone the rest of the night without smoking and not regretted it.

The patience needed to stalk human quarry was something Longarm had learned long ago.

Chapter 31

Longarm turned his head to the left and squinted. The sun was half an hour off the horizon and still there was no sound of movement from inside the soddy. And still smoke continued to drift out from beneath the sapling supported eaves of the house.

Longarm didn't like that. A fire should have had to be replenished hours ago. But surely he would have heard if the man inside pawed through a wood box or clanged a stove door.

No one had approached through the night, and nothing but the burro moved close by.

Off to the south Longarm could see his own roan staked out on the grass. That and a stream of droning flies were the only living things in view.

He stood and walked around the place, avoiding only the east-facing wall with its doorway, but he saw nothing for miles in any direction.

If Adamson was inside, or Warren, surely he should be awake by now.

Longarm set the Winchester butt down on the ground and leaned it against the eastern wall of the soddy. The Colt would be preferable at close range if there was trouble inside. He slid the Thunderer into his palm and paused for a moment at the buffalo-robe door.

Then quick and hard he burst through and to the side, Colt held at the ready.

"Shit!" he complained loudly.

He came out of his keyed-up crouch and shoved the Colt back into the leather.

No wonder he hadn't heard anyone moving inside the soddy the whole damned night long.

The sole occupant of the crude little home lay faceup on the floor between the fireplace and a rickety table.

It didn't take much guesswork to see that this man was not going to make any noises ever again. Not unless his coffin bumped and clattered when it was lowered into the ground.

Warren Adamson, or maybe Ambrose Warren, was stony cold dead.

Longarm cursed some more and looked around before he went to the body.

Whoever killed the wolfer had tried to fire the house too. That was the smoke that had guided Longarm here and that he'd been smelling the whole rest of the night.

The cot and bedding in one corner of the place had burned and still smoldered, but the roof poles hadn't caught fire even though he could see four different places where some-one had tried to light them.

A pile of furs in a front corner was unmolested. In another corner there was a jumble of traps of various sizes, and a battered old front-loading Springfield rifle hung on pegs over the doorway.

Two open-fronted crates piled one on top of another served as shelving, countertop, and cabinetry all rolled into one. The owner of the place hadn't been one to surround himself with luxuries.

Longarm frowned and strode across the small room to stare down at the dead man.

It wasn't a pretty sight.

He'd taken a shotgun blast in the face at very close range. There just wasn't a hell of a lot left there to look at.

Longarm knelt beside the body.

Was this the mortal remains of Ambrose Warren?

The description was certainly right. Including what little Longarm could see of the corpse's features. The hair color was right, and there was a balding patch high on the back of the head. Longarm remembered clearly that Brose Warren had had such a bald spot. A little smaller than this when Longarm had seen it. But then that had been years ago too. It stood to reason that the size of the spot would have grown over the years Warren spent in prison.

The face would have told the story for sure, of course.

But there wasn't any face left to look at. That all had gone away under a hail of shotshell pellets. The whole front of the dead man's skull was either carried away or crushed in.

Longarm picked up the dead man's hands and examined them. The nails were bitten and chewed and the hands none too clean.

There was no hideout derringer riding under the right sleeve where Longarm remembered Warren carrying one. But that meant nothing. The rig Longarm remembered would have been confiscated years back. Warren might not have replaced it, or might simply have chosen not to wear it in the safety of his own home.

His pockets turned up only a few coins, a filthy bandanna, and a folding Barlow knife that had been whetted thin from countless sharpenings.

The body was able to tell him too damned little.

Longarm stood, his knee joints popping, and began snooping through the dead man's personal effects.

A cigar box on one shelf held bottles of trap-bait scents. Longarm knew better than to open any of those. The primary ingredient in most trap lures was skunk piss. And went downhill from there.

150

There were some staple foods, mostly coarsely ground cornmeal. Two pots, two spoons, one fork. A little salt and some rank-smelling grease in a tin can. The man hadn't lived high on the hog.

On the other hand, if this had been the boar's nest of Ambrose Warren, he might not have *lived* here at all. Just set this place up as a cover, much like Longarm's own fabricated tale of being an innocent cowman looking for ground to graze his beeves.

The soddy wasn't newly built like the ones on the farms Longarm had been visiting, but that meant little. Warren could have taken it over from a real hermit and trapper, or simply found it already sitting here and decided to make use of it.

Longarm frowned and continued his search.

There seemed to be nothing to point a finger at the identity of the dead man on the floor.

He dug through the remains of the bedding that had been set afire and found a small cache of five- and ten-dollar gold coins and the heat-twisted remains of an old locket made of cheap gilt. The locket was warped closed and would not open easily. Longarm used the point of the dead man's Barlow to pry it open, damn near cutting himself in the process. The knife was mighty sharp.

The effort hadn't been worth his trouble. There had been a painted miniature inside the locket, but the heat of the fire had made the colors melt and run so it was impossible to see anything of what the face had been. There was no engraving inside the locket case, which was what Longarm had been hoping for.

He examined the pile of traps and found nothing there. Emptied a box of buffalo chips and found nothing but dried buffalo shit to be used for fuel.

There was nothing on the table and nothing hidden in the fireplace ashes nor underneath the hearthstone.

Two shirts and a buffalo coat were hung on pegs, but there was nothing in the pockets of any of the garments.

He went so far as to pull the dead man's shoes off and check inside them. Nothing there, although he did find a folded five-dollar bill stuffed inside the man's right sock.

He sighed. About all that was left in the place was the pile of dried furs in the front corner.

No sense in starting a job and not carrying through with it. He squatted beside the furs and began lifting them and setting them aside one by one.

"Well, now," he said as he neared the bottom. "What do we have here?"

A man's suit of clothes had been carefully folded and laid flat, then hidden underneath the stack of furs.

"Well, now indeed."

Would a reclusive old wolfer be likely to keep a new suit of clothes on hand?

Damned improbable.

And the suit was definitely quite new. Cheap cloth and construction, true, but showing very little wear.

It occurred to Longarm that Billy Vail had mentioned something about Brose Warren serving out his prison term and being released with a coin and a new suit of clothes.

This suit of clothes?

Damn sure could be. The drab color and cheap cut were what a prison might issue. The white shirt and patent collar folded together with the suit were as cheap as the suit was. The shirt smelled of sweat and of sizing. It had never been washed.

Longarm stood and went through the pants pockets. They were empty. He tried again with the coat.

And smiled.

In the right hand coat pocket there was a pasteboard stub of a railway ticket.

The ticket had been issued by the Denver and Rio Grande, good for taking the passenger from Canon City to Denver.

Bingo!

Canon City was the site of the state prison where Ambrose Warren had served his time.

And Denver likely was just about as far as a freed prisoner's release money could carry him on the D&RG.

How the SOB would have gotten from there to here, and why here in particular, was anybody's guess.

So was the question of who killed him and why.

Longarm walked over to the body again and stared down at it.

Ambrose Warren and the bad end he'd been rushing toward all his life?

It was certainly possible. Perhaps even likely at this point. That suit of prison clothes was the giveaway. The rest of this soddy and trapper shit was so much window dressing.

But if this corpse was Ambrose Warren, where were his partners and what had become of the loot he'd taken from Beck City?

Longarm went back to the pile of furs and finished pulling the last of them away, but there was nothing more to find. If anything else was hidden inside the soddy, the hider had done a fine job of concealing it.

He took one last look at the body and walked back outside into the cleaner air there.

The burro wouldn't be strong enough to carry a dead man back to town. Longarm figured he could tell Jeff Barnes about it and let him send someone out to collect the remains for burial.

The burro gave him a soft-cyed, hopeful look, and he drew a bucket of water from the hand-dug well for it, then pulled the gate poles down so it could get out to grass after it drank. It would be cruel to leave it penned like this with no one alive at the place to tend to its needs.

Then Longarm retrieved his Winchester and began walking back to the picketed roan.

He was hungry, he realized now. He wouldn't be especially welcome at the cafe in town, but he could buy some supplies from another merchant and make do.

His stride lengthened as he got to thinking about food, and he put the roan into a lope for Beck City as soon as he was in the saddle again.

Chapter 32

Longarm stepped inside the bank, caught the teller's eye, and hooked a thumb in the direction of the small room where the Beck City post office was located. The teller glanced past the shoulder of a man at his window and nodded, holding one finger upraised to tell Longarm he would be there in a minute.

Longarm had letters ready to post to Billy Vail and to the Lakeside National Protective Association.

Before the teller finished with his customer, a smiling Andy Beck came out of an office door at the back of the bank and motioned for Longarm to join him.

Beck's office was as grand as his home, if on a considerably smaller scale. The paintings on the walls were excellent even to Longarm's untutored eye, and were probably expensive as well. The rug on his floor was Persian, and the desk was probably worth more than a deputy marshal earned in a year's time. If money was what interested a man, banking was definitely preferable to carrying a badge for a living.

"Good news," Beck said happily.

"Oh, what?"

Andy Beck laughed and motioned Longarm to a seat in a leather-upholstered armchair. "Your news, Longarm, not mine. Jeff told me you found your man this morning."

"Thanks t' you," Longarm told the pleasant young banker.

"I'm delighted I was able to be of help. The only regret I have is that now you won't still be here for the wedding. Loretta will be disappointed about that. She is quite fond of you, you know."

"She's a nice girl." He smiled. "Lady, I should say now. You're a lucky man, Andy."

"And don't I know it." The banker beamed with pleasure. "There isn't anything I wouldn't do for Loretta."

"Long as she has you t' care for her an' be with her, Andy, i'm sure she'll be as happy as she is now."

Beck smiled. "Perhaps we can have another party before you leave, Longarm. I'm sure Loretta would enjoy that. She told me over and over at breakfast this morning . . . please understand, Longarm, that Loretta and I are sharing the house until the ceremony but not, um . . . "

"You don't owe me any explanations, Andy. 'Specially concerning Miss Day's morals. She's gentle and fine as they come." It occurred to him that in a few more weeks, Miss Day would be dropping the phrase "my fiancé Mr. Beck" just as she'd dropped "my fiancé Mr. Moresbeck." That would undoubtedly be a relief for everyone around her. But then probably not everyone found it as grating as Longarm did.

"Thank you, Longarm. As I was saying, I can't tell you how many times Loretta said how much she enjoyed our get-together last night."

"So did I," Longarm assured him.

Beck motioned for someone outside the office door to join them, and a moment later the bank teller came in. "Yes, sir?"

"I believe Mr. Long has some letters to mail, Kent. Would you take them for him, please."

"Yes, sir."

Longarm relinquished his mail to the teller.

"Was there anything else, sir?"

"No, Kent, that will do."

The teller left, and Andy Beck held Longarm in conversation there for the better part of the next hour, most of that time rhapsodizing about his plans for the marriage ceremony. The musicians were being brought all the way from St. Louis; an outdoor gazebo was being built in Great Falls and would be shipped down in advance of the date, and the minister would be the Methodist bishop in charge of all of Montana Territory. It would be quite the affair, Longarm conceded without a great deal of genuine interest. While Beck rattled on in his excitement, Longarm turned his thoughts to other matters.

"You know," Longarm said at length, "I just might hang around here a spell longer. If I stretch things out long enough, why, I might could stay until the wedding and see you two hitched."

Andy Beck acted like he thought that was the second-best news he'd ever heard, the best, of course, being Miss Day's acceptance of his marriage proposal.

"Why, I can't wait to see Loretta's happiness when I tell her that news," he said enthusiastically.

"Best not say anything to her yet," Longarm cautioned. "After all, I have a boss who might not agree to letting me stay. Let's see how things work out before you make any promises 'bout it."

"However you think best," Beck agreed.

They chatted a little longer, and then Longarm ambled back out onto the street. He went down to the smithy to reclaim the roan and started out toward the farms once again.

Chapter 33

"Sure, I know a fella like that. Could be your friend. Fella name of Warren Adamson. But I hear he's dead now, sorry."

Funny, but that was *exactly* the response—oh, not in the same precise wording from one time to the next, but certainly the same general content of the answers to his questions—that Longarm had been getting now from one end of the street to the other.

Everywhere he stopped, everyone he questioned invariably knew Warren Adamson, and moreover was sure that this Adamson was Mr. Long's old acquaintance from Colorado.

Longarm had started out to collect his horse at Clete Miller's smithy, but still hadn't gotten that far. He'd started talking to folks along the way. And kept getting these same answers in every shop and store he entered.

For a recluse, he reflected, this Adamson fella had got around a whole lot.

Everybody in Beck City knew him.

No, they admitted, they hadn't known Adamson well. But they'd seen him in town at least once every week or sometimes more.

And yes, he sure did fit that description Mr. Long was giving, buck teeth and bald spot and everything.

No, he wasn't known to carry any sort of pistol. Not out in the open anyway. A merchant named Cornwall said he thought he'd seen a lump in Adamson's pocket once that might have been a pistol, but he wasn't sure about that. Everyone else spoke only of the man's rifle, sometimes carried and sometimes not.

Longarm frowned and smoked and carefully, thoroughly worked both sides of the business street of Beck City from end to end.

He spoke with everyone he could find, including a close-mouthed and embarrassed Troy Tate. Longarm decided that talking with one member of the Tate family was enough, though. He didn't go into the cafe side of the place and didn't run into underaged and oversexed Marta while he was talking with her dad. He wouldn't say that he was disappointed to have missed seeing the girl again.

Finally, hours after he had expected to do so, he reached the smithy.

The friendly blacksmith greeted him with a smile. "Hullo, Custis. You look . . ." Miller paused to search for the word he wanted. "Puzzled?"

Longarm shrugged. "Curious 'bout something, Clete."

"An' what would that be, Custis?"

"Oh, it's just that I've been asking for a man I used to know down home. And today all of a sudden everybody's telling me who he is an' where I can find him. Except today he's dead, so that I can't go talk to him myself and see if he's the fella I'm looking for."

Miller nodded and used his tongs to rearrange a bit of glowing-hot iron on his coals. He set the tongs down and reached up to give a tug on the bellows handle, then fished in his pocket for a plug of tobacco. Longarm shook his head when a chew was offered.

"Warren Adamson, that would be," Miller said without Longarm ever getting around to asking the question.

"How'd you know that?"

The smith grinned. "This here's a small town, Custis. Everybody knows by now that you're a Ewe Ess marshal come to arrest Adamson for something. An' know also that the old boy got himself shot down last night before you could get to 'im and get 'im to talk about his accomplices."

"Nobody said . . ."

Miller's grin got wider. "Course they didn't. You didn't outright ask. That'd be because you're still pretending to be a cowman. Am I right?"

It was Longarm's turn to grin. He chuckled and acknowledged that Miller had it right.

"Hell, Custis, these are good folks here. They're tryin' t' be helpful an' not embarrass you by lettin' the cat outa the bag about knowin' who you really are."

"Damn," Longarm swore. Sometimes a man could just plain outsmart himself when he tried to get sneaky.

He found it interesting, though, that the townspeople now believed that Adamson had been behind their troubles but also understood that there had to have been accomplices involved too. The troubles in Beck City hadn't ended with Adamson's death.

"Do you want my two cents worth on what I know 'bout old Warren?"

"Of course, Clete."

"Truth is, Custis, I probably knew the man better than anybody else in town. He'd come in here every now an' then. Always the same routine, an' always stopped here at my place first thing. That's because I used to tend his burro for him. He'd always bring Timothy here for me to look after."

"Timothy," Longarm repeated.

"That's the burro's name."

"Timothy is a mare," Longarm mentioned.

"Yeah, but all Warren's burros were named Timothy. This Timothy was the seventh or eighth he'd had by that name, I think he said, and every one of them since the first named after his brother. Warren said he called the first one that because his brother was an ass too, but then he got to like the burros and decided maybe his brother hadn't been so bad after all. Anyhow . . . "

Longarm scowled, but Miller didn't notice and kept up his line of prattle. "Anyhow, Warren would come by here an' leave Timothy for me to take care of, then he'd go over to the stage office with his furs. Shipped them someplace to sell them, but I couldn't tell you where. I expect Don Regvald at the company office would know."

Longarm had already talked with Regvald, but the man hadn't volunteered information that wasn't specifically requested.

"Once his furs were bundled ready for shipment . . . shipped 'em with the freight charges collect, I think he told me once . . . he'd go over to the post office an' pick up his mail. Which was always the money he'd been paid for his last shipment of furs. Never anything else. He used to complain sometimes that his damn brother Timothy never wrote to him. Not that Warren ever wrote to Timothy either, mind, but it used to gravel him. But he always had his money waiting for him from his furs.

"Then he'd stop in the bank to cash his check an' take it over to the whorehouse. He'd hold one dollar back from whatever he earned. He'd put that away in a separate pocket, see, an' the next day I'd collect the ten cents he owed me for keeping Timothy and give him back the change he was due. Everything else he'd be free to spend if he wanted, however much it was. Though he did tell me once that he was gettin' old enough now that he had money left over from his drinking and carousing more often than not. Used to bother him that he couldn't screw but a few times in one night anymore. Said when he was a young buck he could spend more on whores than he could earn. Bothered him something awful when he found he was able t' earn more'n he could fuck away."

Longarm smiled. Then quickly became serious. "How long have you been in this country, Clete?"

"Since early May of last year. I came in sooner than most

160

but not as early as some. I'm no farmer, so I bought one of the town lots and set up in trade. Never was formally apprenticed, mind, but I like the work and picked it up here and there. It's a pleasure bein' able to do something that I like an' make a living at it."

"And Adamson? Do you know if he was here very long?"

Miller shrugged. "That kinda depends on what you think a long time is, don't it? I'd call it long. Maybe you wouldn't."

"And your idea of a long time would be . . . ?"

"What Warren told me . . . an' I got no way to verify this, you understand, as I sure as hell wasn't in this country at the time . . . but what Warren told me was that he come out to the mountains early in the sixties . . . didn't say exactly that he was avoiding conscription, but that's the assumption a fella kinda naturally makes . . . and tried prospecting in the Black Hills, tried again in the Absarokas, even went clear on over into the Bitterroots. Tried placer mining for a while. Drew wages on a dredge. Finally quit trying to get rich looking for gold and went to trading furs with the Blackfoot. Sold out his trading post to a man named Schultz and went to trapping for himself. Learned the trapping from an old-timer named Beckworth. Even went down into Wyoming and talked to that Jim Bridger fella at his store there before the old man died. Then got run out o' that country by the Mormons an' came back up here. Been here ever since, he said, taking wolf an' coyote pelts and buffalo before the herds was all shot out." Miller turned his head and spat. "Me, I'd call that a long time, Custis."

Longarm grunted. He happened to agree with Clete's judgment on that subject.

But that wasn't at all what he was thinking about right now.

The only kind of quarry Ambrose Warren had ever in his life trapped, least as far as Custis Long knew about, was human. The man was a sonuvabitch and a hardcase but no kind of outdoorsman.

And Ambrose Warren was released from the Canon City prison just three months ago.

No way were Ambrose Warren and Warren Adamson one and the same man.

"You've been a mighty big help, Clete. Bigger'n you know."

"Glad to hear that, Marshal."

"Deputy," Longarm corrected automatically. He smiled. "But still Custis to you, Clete. Or Longarm if you prefer. That's what most of my friends call me."

"I'll stick with Custis since that's what I already know you as. Anyway I can help, Custis, you just let me know."

"You already have," Longarm assured the smith. He turned toward his roan and glanced toward the sun overhead. He still had some hours of daylight to work with and still wanted to talk to more of the farmers in the area. It would be easier now, he realized. Now that there was no longer any point to pretending he was other than what he really was.

He saddled the horse quickly and put it into a lope toward the country to the north.

Chapter 34

One good thing. A man asking questions in farm country didn't have to worry about going hungry while he was doing it. His only problem in that regard was trying to fend off all the goodies that were forced onto him. And those farm wives could damn sure cook. Dried apricot pie was something a fella couldn't easily turn down even if his belly was already groaning.

Longarm wiped his mouth on the back of his hand and refused the offer of another cup of coffee, then stood. "I thank you for trying to help," he told Mr. and Mrs. Jenks. "And for that pie. That was as good as I've ever tasted, ma'am." The lady blushed.

"I'll walk you out to your horse, Marshal," Jenks offered.

"While you're out there, Gerald, fetch me back a pail of water. Don't be wasting the trip. And don't be lollygagging out there too long. I have scraps for you to take out to the pigs and trash to be burned too. Too much to be done around here for you to be lazing about, Gerald Jenks."

She handed him the bucket and got back a frown.

"Bossy old woman," Jenks complained once the two men were out of earshot from the house.

"Fine cook, your woman," Longarm said with diplomatic truthfulness.

"Ayuh, she can cook all right." Jenks patted his belly, which protruded a good distance over his belt buckle despite the hard physical labor he engaged in from dawn to dusk nearly every day of his life. "I'll give her that much. Chew?" He offered his plug to the guest.

"No, thanks. I prefer these." Longarm pulled out a cheroot, nipped the tip off and spat it out, then struck a match. He got a coal going, then reached for the reins that he'd wrapped around a hitch ring bolted to a post near the Jenkses' sod shed.

"Before you go, Marshal . . . "

"Deputy. Just a deputy." Longarm smiled. "Though I thank you for the promotion."

"Whatever." The farmer looked over his shoulder to make sure his wife hadn't come outside where she might overhear. "Before you leave, Deputy, there's something I oughta mention to you."

"Yes?"

"About this man you're looking for?"

"Warren. Ambrose Warren. You know him?"

"Not by that name, Marshal. Deputy, I mean. But I know a man looks something like that."

Longarm let the reins go slack and quit thinking about stepping up onto that saddle. Mr. Jenks had his full attention now.

"Buck teeth like a jackrabbit," Jenks said. "But he don't have only a bald spot back of his head, he's bald all over. Just a mite of fringe left. More hair coming outa his nose than is left on top of his head. I believe you mentioned, though, that it's been a while since you've seen this Warren. A man gets balder and balder once it starts. Happens quick too. Trust me. I know." Jenks pulled his hat off and ran his palm over a scalp that was as naked as a baby's butt.

"I hadn't thought about that," Longarm admitted. "And it's been a good while now. I suppose he could have gone the rest of the way bald since I saw him last."

"Fella with a head o' hair like yours, Marshal . . . Deputy . . . he doesn't realize how quick a man's hair can go. Five, six years is all it took me once I started losing it."

The descriptions Longarm had been giving right along were all for a man with protruding teeth and a small bald spot at the back of a head of dark brown hair. He had to concede that Jenks could be right. Perhaps by now Longarm was looking for a bald man with buck teeth.

"Look, uh, if I say any more about this . . . you don't have to, uh . . . you don't have to tell anybody where you heard it from, do you?" Jenks added nervously.

"Of course not, Mr. Jenks. If you're worried about me dragging you away from your crops to testify in a court of law somewhere . . . "

"Hell, that isn't it. Comes to that, Marshal . . . Deputy . . . I'd be pleased for the excuse to get away on a trip for a change. No, what I'm wanting you to keep quiet is, well, I oughtn't to ever have seen this fella that I'm talking about. I'd just as soon nobody, and in particular my old woman back there . . . I'd just as soon nobody ever had to know where you got this information from. If you see what I mean."

Longarm didn't particularly, but he was quick to reassure Jenks that no one had to know his source of information. "Confidentiality is normal in my line of work, Mr. Jenks. The only person other than you and me who ever has to hear about this is my boss. And he's all the way down in Denver. I can promise you neither of us will ever discuss this with your wife, whatever you may have to tell me."

Jenks hesitated a moment longer, then shuffled closer and lowered his voice. "This man calls himself Abner Wiggins. He runs the whorehouse outside Beck City. I . . . well, never mind how I know him. If you see what I mean."

This time Longarm saw. Mr. Jenks liked to get himself a little strange pussy now and then and didn't want the wife to know about it.

165

"Abner Wiggins," Longarm repeated. Ambrose Warren. More often than not, it sometimes seemed, a man would stick with his own initials when he chose an alias for himself. It could fit.

"That's right. Bald as an eagle and with teeth out to here." Jenks held a hand up in front of his face. "I'm not saying that Wiggins is your man, mind. But it just might could be him."

"I'll look into it. Thanks."

"Glad to help if I can. Just don't . . . "

"I won't," Longarm promised. "You have my word on it."

Jenks looked relieved.

The two men shook hands, and Longarm mounted the roan. He glanced toward the sinking sun and turned the animal's nose back toward Beck City. He should get there, he figured, just past sundown. That ought to be just about right for the town whorehouse to be opening for its evening trade.

Just about right for him to have a word with Mr. Abner Wiggins.

Chapter 35

"Sorry, we aren't open for business. Weekends only, mister."

Longarm looked at the woman who had finally responded to his repeated hammering on the whorehouse door.

She was slender and not terribly bad-looking, but she wasn't nearly as young as she tried to appear under her layers of powder and rouge. Perhaps as old as forty, he decided, but you would have to look close to see it. Mostly it showed in the wrinkles on the backs of her hands and on her neck. She wore a thin chemise, black stockings, and apparently little or nothing else.

"That's all right," he told her. "I'm not here to do business with you. Not your business, anyhow." He pulled out his wallet and flipped it open, exposing his badge.

"Go away. This ain't your jurisdiction. Jeff Barnes takes care of things here."

Longarm grinned. "Now isn't it interesting that you're all prepared with jurisdictional arguments, and all I want to do is sit down and talk with the girls here."

"Fuck you," she said and pushed the door closed. Tried to anyway. Longarm's boot wedged between it and the door frame prevented it.

"Thought I already told you that I wasn't here for that," he said agreeably.

She glared down at the boot, then gave in to the inevitable with a shrug and a frown. She pulled the door open and motioned him inside. "Make this quick, will you?"

"Glad to," he agreed.

He removed his hat and carefully wiped his feet on a throw rug at the entry, then stepped into the parlor.

The place was empty and silent, with only a single lamp burning. "Busy, aren't you?" he observed.

"I told you already, we're closed except on weekends."

"Business is that bad?"

"Is that what you came here to talk about? If so I think you can turn right around and leave. There's no law I know of that says I have to tell you about my trade. And I don't keep any records, so don't bother asking to see them and don't bother trying to subpoena them. There aren't any for you to look at."

"I want to talk with Mr. Wiggins," Longarm said.

"Never heard of him," the whore said.

Longarm smiled happily. "Thank you. You have now committed a misdemeanor, and I can arrest you if I feel it's necessary."

"Up yours, asshole."

"You do insist on pushing it, don't you. First you perjure yourself by giving false information to a peace officer conducting an official investigation, then you commit a verbal assault. Or slander. We could call that one slander, I think. Not that you're looking at very much time, of course. Call it six months on each charge. I know a friendly judge who would go for that and make the terms consecutive instead of concurrent. You'll be out in a year, easy." There pretty much had to be a federal judge in Montana Territory, of course, but the truth was that Longarm had no idea in the world who the man might be. As for making silly charges like that stick . . .

The woman frowned, which really was about all he'd hoped to accomplish. "Why don't we start over, dearie." She smiled and sat on a once-plush but now badly faded couch and pulled him down to a seat beside her. Her hand fell high on the inside of his thigh, and she shifted closer so that her hip was pressed warm against his. "How can I help you, Deputy?" No misunderstanding here about his precise title and duties.

No misunderstanding either about the level of bullshit he could expect from this woman.

"I want to see Mr. Wiggins."

"Mr. Wiggins is not available at the moment. He's gone to Great Falls on business."

"I see. Thank you."

She slid her hand a little higher. He reached down, took her by the wrist, and moved the hand over into her own lap. The front of her chemise had slipped down so her breasts were exposed all the way to the tops of her nipples. That didn't seem to bother her anymore than it was bothering him.

"Your name?" he asked.

"LuLu."

"Your real name?"

"LuLu," she repeated. "LuLu Smith."

"How many girls are working here, LuLu Smith?"

She hesitated, probably realized he could find out easily enough on his own by asking in town, and said, "There are only two of us."

"And the other girl?"

"French Annie."

"Jones?"

"However did you guess," she said without bothering to hide her smirk.

"LuLu and French Annie. All right. Where is French Annie now?"

"Sleeping."

"Of course. And Mr. Wiggins is in Great Falls."

"That's right."

"Who else works here?"

"Nobody. That's all of us. Just us three."

"Wiggins and two girls, that isn't much to run a place this size."

"I already told you business hasn't gotten good yet. We expect to expand when it does."

"Of course. Mind if I smoke?"

"Not at all, dearie."

He lit up.

LuLu Smith stood and went over to a cabinet set against the side wall. She lifted the lid, exposing a set of bottles and glassware. "Care for a drink to go with that, dearie?" Without waiting for an answer she picked up one of the unlabeled decanters and poured a generous shot into a small glass, then carried it over to him.

"Thanks." There was no point in being stuffy now. Not that he really expected to learn anything from this woman either way. And he'd been looking forward to having a drink later anyway. He raised the glass in a silent salute and tried it. His eyebrows went up. The whiskey was rye, his preference, and not a bad brand.

"Is that all right, dearie?"

"Fine."

"You want to fuck too? No charge, honey." She slipped the chemise off her shoulders. For a woman her age she had nice tits, and her belly didn't sag.

"No thanks. I'll finish my drink and my smoke and go."

"Whatever you want, dearie."

They sat in complete silence while Longarm sipped at the rye whiskey.

His attention was keenly attuned, but he could hear no hint of movement anywhere in the place outside this parlor. The whorehouse might have been a tomb for all the life that was in it at the moment.

LuLu Smith didn't bother to cover herself, and Longarm didn't want to give her the satisfaction of suggesting it. He ignored her while she sat and watched him peacefully finish first the whiskey and then his cheroot.

"Come by anytime," she said when he stood.

"Thank you."

Longarm walked back the way he had come in. The outside door led into a foyer that had the parlor door leading off it to the left, another door standing half open on the right, and a hallway winding back into the interior of the low, sprawling whorehouse.

When he left the parlor instead of turning right to go out the front door, he angled off to his left, into the hallway.

"Hey! You can't go back there," LuLu Smith shouted.

"Whatever you say," he agreed. "Dearie." And continued on down the hall.

Chapter 36

"Watch out! He's coming!"

LuLu Smith sounded like she was running away, but that wasn't what Longarm was listening for now.

There!

Bed springs creaked and feet hit the floor somewhere a few rooms ahead of him.

He let his ears guide the way and slammed a shoulder into the door.

The flimsy wood splintered, and the door crashed open.

He could see a man's backside disappearing out a small window, but there was no time to be thinking about him now.

There was another figure in the room, and all Longarm could see of it in that first rush was the fact that it was holding a short-barreled carbine.

He dropped to the floor and rolled as a lance of flame licked across the room searching for flesh. Searching with the bullet that was its spearhead.

He spun off to the side and came up again with the Thunderer in his hand and spitting fire and smoke right back.

The woman with the carbine—French Annie, it had to be—took his slug full in the chest and fell backward onto the bed she'd just vacated.

French Annie was naked and middle-aged and in death looked small and wrinkled and ugly.

A small red dot between her breasts began to leak blood.

The short-barreled carbine—a .32-20 boy's model, he guessed—lay on the floor where she'd dropped it when Longarm's bullet put her down.

He didn't have time at the moment to worry about the fact that he'd just killed a woman.

Right now the man who'd been with her was of paramount importance.

Longarm came off the floor in a rush and dove for the window.

Behind him there was another crash of sound as someone else, LuLu he assumed, got off a hurried shot that came nowhere near him.

He sailed through the open window like a diver slicing into water, tucked his shoulder, and rolled when he hit the ground.

It was nearly full dark, but he could hear running footsteps in the distance.

Longarm scrambled to his feet and began legging it in pursuit of the man who was behind all this.

It had to be Ambrose Warren, dammit. Had to be. And Warren had been calling himself Abner Wiggins here.

Longarm stretched his legs and quickly closed the gap on the fleeing Warren.

He had the man's back in sight now in the last, lingering traces of the twilight. The moon wouldn't rise for hours, but no matter. Now that Longarm had the son of a bitch in view he wasn't going to lose him again.

Two hundred yards, three . . . Warren was nearly close enough to tackle.

Warren must have heard how near his pursuer had come. He threw his hands high into the air and slowed, puffing

173

and out of breath after the chase.

"I . . . give up . . . don't . . . shoot. I quit."

Longarm stopped where he was, half a dozen paces behind Warren, and held the Colt aimed at the small of the man's back.

French Annie had been undressed, but Brose Warren wasn't. He was fully clothed and was wearing, Longarm noticed, a long-sleeved shirt with loose cuffs.

Just like the last time.

Surely the man wasn't going to be stupid enough to try the same trick again.

"Give it up, Brose."

"That you, Longarm?"

"Yes, it is."

"I shoulda got away first thing when I heard you were around, damn you. Thought I could lay low and you'd leave once you thought I was dead already."

"It's another murder charge on you, Brose, for that poor old trapper."

Warren shrugged. "So what's one more, Longarm? They can't hang a guy but once."

"I suppose you're right."

"Okay if I turn around now? I won't try anything, I promise."

"Do whatever you like, Brose," Longarm told him.

Warren turned to face his captor and shrugged again.

"Damn, you have gone bald, haven't you. I almost wouldn't have recognized you."

"Prison didn't much agree with me, Longarm. Hardly know what to do with a real pussy after all these years of fucking my own hand. I got to say, though, that you've done all right by yourself. Dried up some behind your ears since I saw you that time. You've got yourself quite a reputation in Canon City."

"I didn't know that, Brose. Thanks for the compliment."

"It wasn't exactly meant as a compliment, dammit. Lots of boys in there would like to face you."

"I'll take it as one anyhow. And as for facing me, anyone of them is welcome to try. You were too, Brose, but I don't remember you being in any hurry for the two of us to stand face to face."

"What I shoulda done was pop you long range from ambush."

"That's been tried too."

The bald, aging ex-con chuckled. "Had the drop on you once though, didn't I? You can't know how much ragging I had to live with for that damn misfire." He shook his head and sighed. "I sure do miss that little spring rig. Never been able to find another one like it."

"Maybe you should have asked the court to return it."

"Maybe I should have at that. Hell, maybe this time I will."

"Figure to live that long do you, Brose?"

"Aw, a good lawyer will get me twenty. With good behavior that lets me out in ten. I can do that. Won't like it, mind, but I can do it."

"With your testimony about your women?" Longarm suggested.

"If that's what it takes. You want to work a deal with me, Longarm?"

"You know I don't have any authority to bargain with you, Brose."

"You could put a word in for me. I know that much. You play it straight, Longarm. They say that about you too. And those women, they don't mean more to me than my neck does. They were in on this with me. All of it. Dressed like men part of the time and like women sometimes. Both of them can shoot well enough. They're the ones killed that insurance fella from Chicago. I wasn't with them that day because you were in town and I was already laying low. They done that one on their own. That information ought to buy me something, shouldn't it?"

"Annie's dead," Longarm mentioned, deliberately avoiding the making of any promises that a prosecutor might not want to honor. "I shot her back there at the whorehouse. By now LuLu should be hoofing it for elsewhere."

"But you'll tell them I came clean with you, right? You'll tell them what I told you?"

"I'll tell them about this conversation, yes."

"Can I put my hands down now, Longarm? My arms are getting kinda tired."

"You do whatever you want, Brose." The man's sleeves had slipped down onto his forearms while he held his hands raised. Longarm could see that this time Brose Warren really didn't have a spring rig strapped on him.

"Thanks." Warren brought his arms down and made a face. "I swear I'm getting too old for this shit, Longarm. Glad this is the last time I'll have to face you." He rubbed his right bicep and sighed. "That feels better." He reached across with his right hand to massage the other bicep too.

Longarm triggered the Colt. The heavy slug crunched through flesh and bone, and Ambrose Warren gave Longarm a look of incredulity. He staggered backward, caught himself, and managed to keep his feet.

"Shit, you *have* grown up, haven't you?"

Then he toppled face forward. The body hit the ground with a thump and never so much as bounced.

A tiny derringer dropped free onto the dirt. He'd been hiding it in his shirt pocket and palmed it when he was pretending to ease his muscles.

"Yeah," Longarm said softly. "But you never did."

He shucked the empties out of the Thunderer, reloaded the revolver, and began walking back to the whorehouse.

By now LuLu Smith was probably long gone, but he would have to see that for himself just to make sure.

Chapter 37

Longarm nodded to the bank teller and pointed toward the office in the back.

"I'll tell him you're here, Marshal." The teller hurried to the bank president's office, paused to tap on the closed door, and then opened it. A moment later a grinning Andy Beck came out with his hand extended. He grabbed Longarm's hand and pumped it.

"Wonderful work, Longarm. Wonderful. I can't tell you how happy we all are that you've cleaned up our town. Now Beck City can *really* take off and grow. Come inside. I know Loretta will want to offer her congratulations too."

Beck led Longarm inside the private office. Miss Day was already there, seated in the armchair and looking radiantly beautiful in an elegant gown that didn't even try to hide those magnificent breasts.

"Mr. Long. Andy has been telling me what you did last night. I'm so happy for you. And for all of us. My Andy says you've done a great service to this whole town. Thank you."

"My pleasure, Miss Day."

"Is it true what else Andy tells me?"

"Kinda depends on what it is he's told you, doesn't it?"

She laughed. "He said you may stay and attend our wedding, Mr. Long. Is that true?" She didn't give him time to answer. She was so excited that she nearly came out of her chair to tell him, "We've heard from the preacher, Mr. Long, and he will be bringing a choir with him. Little orphaned Indian boys. Can you imagine anything cuter? I can't wait to hear them. And my Andy says he will have an organ shipped in to accompany them and then donate the organ for a church. We'll get started building the church right away. If we have enough workers we might even have it finished in time to hold the ceremony there. Isn't that the most exciting thing you've ever *heard*, Mr. Long?"

Her enthusiasm was touchingly innocent and unaffected. The girl was abubble with joy today.

Longarm gathered too that her stock phrase, "my fiancé Mr. Beck," was to be replaced with "my Andy" in the future.

He sighed. "There's something I expect I ought to tell you, Andy."

"Oh?" Beck pulled another chair close to Miss Day's and motioned Longarm into it, then went around the desk to his own chair. "Whatever it is, Longarm, I'm sure we will be pleased to hear it."

"Uh, don't jump to conclusions too quick, Andy."

"Oh?"

"I've just been over to your jail. Put some folks into it, in fact."

"You caught that woman then. Good."

"No, not her. But I expect she'll show up someplace. I'll have a want put out on her. No, it's your boys the Barnes brothers that I put into the cage, Andy."

Beck frowned and leaned forward. His swivel chair creaked and groaned loudly in the silence that had suddenly come into the bank office. "Jeffrey?"

"Jeff, Danny, and Lute. All of them. To tell you the truth, Andy, I wasn't entirely positive which of them I wanted.

178

Turns out once I had one in cuffs he started pointing fingers."

"But . . . "

"There had t' be somebody else involved, you know. On more'n one of those robberies, there was more than one man along. So it was clear from the start that Brose Warren and his whores weren't acting alone. And I sure knew that you wouldn't go out and do that kind of work yourself, Andy. I have more respect for you than to think that. The Barnes boys were your dogs to kick, so it pretty much had to be at least one of them."

Loretta Day gasped. "Andy? What . . . ?"

Neither Longarm nor Andy Beck was paying much attention to her at the moment, though.

"I can't . . . whatever would make you think, Longarm . . . ?"

"Lots of things, once I got to dragging them all together where I could look at them as all part of one package, Andy."

"But . . . "

"For instance," Longarm went on, "why would Ambrose Warren want to gun down an insurance investigator from Chicago and then not take the time to rob him? Somebody obviously wanted Karl Meek kept from learning anything here, but Warren and his ladies wouldn't have cared. Somebody who was raking in the profits from insured losses would, though. And this bank would be the biggest in that category.

"Then too, Andy, there's the fact that Brose Warren never tried to ambush me. Now I had to wonder about that. It's the way a man like him would normally think. But he never tried it. It occurred to me that he was likely under orders not to. And why might that be? Way I see it, Andy, you didn't want any more federal attention focused here than you already had. If I'd been killed, there would've been a lot more interest in what was happening here. You didn't want that. And I suspect you actually wanted Warren caught. If I hadn't come along to do that job for you, Jeff Barnes would've been told to kill him and clean up the country.

179

You were gonna have to stop the crime wave soon anyway so the town would grow. But not until you had your pile already put aside. A pile which I didn't happen to find anywhere in the whorehouse when I searched it. All that money has to be someplace, and neither Warren nor his women had it.

"Then too, I recall you telling Barnes the other day that you wanted to talk to Abner. Which of course was Brose under another name."

"I talk to—"

"I know, Andy. You talk to just about everybody in town, the local whoremaster included. But Ambrose Warren isn't the one who set that place up and has been running it. He was still in prison when it was built and those girls were brought in. Just another little business enterprise, eh, Andy? So I'd guess it was them you found first and them that pointed you to Brose afterward."

"But . . . "

"The real clincher about it all, though, Andy, was my own name. Which finally occurred to me."

"Your name, Longarm? However would that . . . ?"

Longarm grinned. "My name exactly. Longarm. That's what you called me the other day. Do you remember?"

Beck shrugged.

"*I* do, though I'm so used to hearing it every day that I never paid it much mind at the time. The point is, Andy, I hadn't told that nickname to anybody since before Miss Day and I pulled away from the wharf in Nebraska. Nobody, until I invited Clete Miller to call me that yesterday. But Brose Warren knew it. He knew it from my reputation with his fellow convicts. Then you turned up knowing it too. The only way you could've known that I'm called Longarm is if Ambrose Warren told you. And he wouldn't ever have discussed me with anybody except one of his partners in this deal, Andy."

The banker had gone pale, and his hands were shaking. He made no attempt to hide the fact.

"Andy?" Loretta Day whispered. "Andy, tell him that he's wrong, Andy."

180

"If it makes you feel any better, Miss Day, Andy did everything he did because he loves you. He loves you so much that he wanted to be able to give you everything and knew he couldn't do that on a branch banker's salary. He wanted to give you everything even if he had to steal and murder to do it. He just never understood, you see, that 'everything' to a lady like you is love, that it doesn't have all that much t' do with possessions. Andy got confused on that point, Miss Day. But I think it's fair to say that he honestly does love you."

"Andy!" she protested.

Beck began to cry. He sat trembling and with his eyes downcast while Longarm went behind the handsome desk and pulled out his handcuffs. Andy Beck obediently put his hands behind his back and allowed himself to be put in irons. The meek young man was not the kind to offer physical resistance to his problems. And there was no longer anyone left he could hire to do that for him.

"Let's go, Andy. It's a long way to Helena."

Longarm led him away, leaving a stunned and weeping Loretta Day alone in the bank president's luxurious office.

Watch for

LONGARM IN THE MEXICAN BADLANDS

One hundred forty-seventh in the bold LONGARM series
from Jove

Coming in March!

A special offer for people who enjoy reading the best Westerns published today. If you enjoyed this book, subscribe now and get . . .

TWO FREE

A $5.90 VALUE—NO OBLIGATION

If you enjoyed this book and would like to read more of the very best Westerns being published today, you'll want to subscribe to True Value's Western Home Subscription Service. If you enjoyed the book you just read and want more of the most exciting, adventurous, action packed Westerns, subscribe now.

Each month the editors of True Value will select the 6 very best Westerns from America's leading publishers for special readers like you. You'll be able to preview these new titles as soon as they are published, FREE for ten days with no obligation.

TWO FREE BOOKS

When you subscribe, we'll send you your first month's shipment of the newest and best 6 Westerns for you to preview. With your first shipment, two of these books will be yours as our introductory gift to you absolutely FREE, regardless of what you decide to do. If you like them, as much as we think you will, keep all six books but pay for just 4 at the low subscriber rate of just $2.45 each. If you decide to return them, keep 2 of the titles as our gift. No obligation.

Special Subscriber Savings

When you become a True Value subscriber you'll save money several ways. First, all regular monthly selections will be billed at the low subscriber price of just $2.45 each. That's

WESTERNS!

at least a savings of $3.00 each month below the publishers
price. Second, there is never any shipping, handling or other
hidden charges—Free home delivery. What's more there is no
minimum number of books you must buy, you may return any
selection for full credit and you can cancel your subscription
at any time. A TRUE VALUE!

Mail the coupon below

To start your subscription and receive 2 FREE
WESTERNS, fill out the coupon below and mail it today.
We'll send your first shipment which includes 2 FREE
BOOKS as soon as we receive it.

Mail To:
True Value Home Subscription Services, Inc.   10512
P.O. Box 5235
120 Brighton Road
Clifton, New Jersey 07015-5235

YES! I want to start receiving the very best Westerns being published today.
Send me my first shipment of 6 Westerns for me to preview FREE for 10 days. If I
decide to keep them, I'll pay for just 4 of the books at the low subscriber price of
$2.45 each; a total of $9.80 (a $17.70 value). Then each month I'll receive the 6
newest and best Westerns to preview Free for 10 days. If I'm not satisfied I may
return them within 10 days and owe nothing. Otherwise I'll be billed at the
special low subscriber rate of $2.45 each; a total of $14.70 (at least a $17.70
value) and save $3.00 off the publishers price. There are never any shipping,
handling or other hidden charges. I understand I am under no obligation to
purchase any number of books and I can cancel my subscription at any time, no
questions asked. In any case the 2 FREE books are mine to keep.

Name _____

Address _____ Apt. # _____

City _____ State _____ Zip _____

Telephone # _____

Signature _____
(if under 18 parent or guardian must sign)
Terms and prices subject to change.
Orders subject to acceptance by True Value Home Subscription Services, Inc.